THE Sarah Jane

ADVENTURES

From the makers of Doctor Who

BBC CHILDREN'S BOOKS

Published by the Penguin Group
Penguin Books Ltd, 80 Strand, London WC2R 0RL, England
Penguin Group (USA) Inc., 375 Hudson Street, New York, New York 10014, USA
Penguin Group (Australia) Ltd, 250 Camberwell Road, Camberwell, Victoria, 3124, Australia
(a division of Pearson Australia Group Pty Ltd)
Canada, India, New Zealand, South Africa

Published by BBC Children's Character Books, 2008
Text and design © Children's Character Books, 2008

10 9 8 7 6 5 4 3 2 1

Sarah Jane Adventures © BBC 2007

www.thesja.com

BBC logo ™ & BBC 1996. Licensed by BBC Worldwide Limited

ISBN 978-1-40590-507-7

Printed in Great Britain by Clays Ltd, St Ives plc

THE

Sarah Jane

ADVENTURES

From the makers of Doctor Who
Series created by Russell T Davies

Whatever Happened to Sarah Jane?

Written by Rupert Laight

Based on the script by Gareth Roberts

'I saw amazing things, out there in space. But there's strangeness to be found wherever you turn. Life on Earth can be an adventure, too.

You just have to know where to look.'

SARAH JANE SMITH

Prologue

12th July 1964

'You girls at the back! Sit down this instant!' called Miss Jeffers, in a stern voice. 'We're on a coach, not at the funfair.'

'It's about as near as we'll get to a funfair,' muttered a girl with red hair. She and her brunette friend were sat up front, near the driver. 'Why have we got to visit this stupid old museum anyway?'

'It is a geography field trip, Andrea,' replied the brunette, looking up from her book for a second.

Andrea sighed and glanced out of the window as the coach trundled down a bumpy country road. 'We go all the way to the seaside, and instead of stuffing our faces with candyfloss and having fun on the pier, we have to learn about sedimentary limestone and goodness knows what else!'

She rummaged in her satchel and pulled out a parcel of greaseproof paper containing a corned beef sandwich her mum had made that morning. Andrea contemplated taking a bite, then decided against it and slung the sandwich back in her bag. 'What's the book?' she said, turning to her classmate.

'Oh, nothing interesting.'

'What you reading it for then? Give it here!' And she grabbed the thick hardback and peered at the cover. 'An Unexpurgated History of the Universe,' she read, in a disapproving tone. 'You're right, it is nothing interesting.' She tossed the book back to her friend. 'Still, I wish I was as clever as you. I'm only any good at art, but you get top marks in every class. How do you do it?'

Her friend waved the book at her. 'By keeping my nose stuck in these, of course.'

'Well, if that's the price for good marks, then it's too high for me!'

'Now, class, you have three hours to answer all the questions on the handout,' announced Miss Jeffers. 'That should give you plenty of time to see every exhibit. And for those of you lucky enough to have pocket money, there might even be time for an ice cream in the cafeteria.'

2 H 4 T R F G 8 N D 1 S W O B X O 3 T R 2 U F S 7 K

A wave of excitable chatter rippled through the class, then the kids began slowly filing inside the Westport Geological Museum.

Miss Jeffers pushed her way through the crowd. 'Hurry along now, we haven't got all day,' she called in a bossy voice. 'We have to be back on the coach by two o'clock.' And with that the teacher disappeared inside the museum.

Andrea held on to her friend's cardigan, preventing her from following the others.

'What are you doing?'

'We can have some fun on the front and still have enough time to whip round the museum,' whispered Andrea. 'Come on!' She tugged roughly at her friend's sleeve.

'But we're not meant to. We'll get in trouble.'

'Don't be such a square!' hissed Andrea, and she skipped off with a mischievous laugh.

The brown-haired girl cautiously glanced around, then dashed after her friend.

Although it was July and the air was warm, the sky was overcast and there was a brisk breeze shaking the shop awnings and rustling the brightly coloured flags hanging from the lamp posts that lined the promenade.

Andrea and her friend emerged from the amusement arcade giggling and counting the coins they'd won. They had played on nearly all the penny slot machines and eaten two toffee apples each.

They strolled along the front where old ladies sat on benches snoozing under wide-brimmed hats, where young lovers walked hand in hand, and where the excited screams of children filled the air as they chased one another along the promenade or made sandcastles on the beach.

'What do you want to do when you leave school?' asked the brown-haired girl.

'Make loads and loads of money, marry Ringo Starr and move to Saint-Tropez,' laughed Andrea. 'Why, what do you want to do?'

'Oh, I don't know,' replied her friend. 'Maybe be an explorer, or a famous scientist, or... a journalist.'

'Women can't be journalists!'

'And why not? Women can do anything men can do nowadays. The world's changing, Andrea. And I want to explore it. See everything there is to see.' She paused, her eyes focused on the spot where the sky touches the sea. 'And more.'

'Good luck. I'd be happy with a handsome fella and a semi in Purley.'

There was a long silence.

'We could have a donkey ride.'

'Don't be wet – that's for little kids,' scoffed Andrea. Then an impish look came over her face. 'What we need is a stroll on the pier.'

'But you saw the sign – it's shut for repairs.'

'We can sneak in.' She paused, hands on hips. 'Oh, come on, it'll be a laugh. Better than that crummy museum.'

'But it's dangerous.'

'Dangerous?' mocked Andrea with a snort. 'What's danger to you, Miss Famous Explorer?'

'You're right. Let's do it. It'll be fun. But only ten minutes, then we must go round the museum.'

'You really aren't as much of a teacher's pet as the other girls say,' Andrea smiled warmly. 'I'm so pleased we're friends.' She grabbed hold of her classmate's hand and squeezed it affectionately.

'Thank you, Andrea Yates,' smiled the brunette, as they marched off in the direction of the pier.

'No, thank you... Sarah Jane Smith.'

Chapter One

The faceless one

'Look at me!' yelled Clyde, throwing them a massive, self-congratulating grin as we whizzed by on his skateboard.

Clyde, Maria, Alan, Sarah Jane and Luke were in the skate park. It was a fenced-off area of Ealing Place Park where kids could skateboard without getting in the way of strolling couples, small children playing football, or panting dogs dragging their owners behind them.

Maria sighed. This was typical Clyde, she thought. Always showing off, always trying to prove how cool he was. If he didn't try so hard, he might succeed. Still, deep down, she couldn't help being just a tiny bit impressed. He certainly knew how to skateboard. But she was determined not to let him know that.

When Clyde next zoomed by, a massive grin plastered across his face, Maria just threw him a nonchalant glance, shrugged, and turned to Sarah Jane, who was standing next to her.

'He's good,' said Sarah Jane.

'Yeah, whatever,' responded Maria. But after a few seconds she glanced back at her friend. He'd now disappeared into the dip between two ramps with a screech of tyre rubber. She smiled to herself. 'Okay,' she admitted. 'He's not bad.'

'What is the point of skateboarding?' Luke called out to Clyde. He was standing a little way off, eyeing Clyde's acrobatics with a confused expression.

'With you, there's always got to be a point!' laughed Clyde, and he pulled up beside his friend, using his foot to bring him to a sudden halt. 'It's skateboarding. It's fun.' He shook his head. 'It just is!'

It was obvious that Luke still didn't get it, and he stared, baffled, as Clyde glided off again.

Maria watched as her friend took another turn

around the tarmac-covered course, zoomed up a ramp and flipped elegantly off the end. Very neat, though Maria. Then he pushed his foot down on the back of the board and tried to turn it. This time he wasn't so successful, and the skateboard slipped out to one side and Clyde tumbled clumsily to the ground.

'Careful!' called Sarah Jane, her face immediately dropping into a worried frown.

Maria tutted. 'So Clyde fights Slitheen and Gorgons and that's okay with you, but a bit of skateboarding and you're like whoa!'

Maria thought back to all the adventures she'd had with her new friends. Since she'd moved to Bannerman Road a couple of months ago, her life had changed completely. It had been one crazy, alien-fighting mission after another. First, they'd encountered the treacherous Bane, then the flatulent Slitheen, the ancient Gorgon, and only the other week they'd found themselves aboard an Uvodni spaceship.

'I know!' replied Sarah Jane, sighing and looking a little shamefaced. 'I've changed since I met you lot. I've gone all mumsy.'

'Well, it's a change for the better, if you don't mind me saying,' came a familiar voice from behind.

H 4 T R F G 8 N D 1 S W 0 B X O 3 T R 2 U F S 7 K

Maria's dad, Alan, was walking towards them. 'Do you remember that day we moved in?' he asked, smiling at Sarah Jane. 'Talk about frosty!'

'I was not!' she protested.

'Yes, you were!' chuckled Maria.

Just then everyone turned in Clyde's direction. He'd let out a yell and was down on the ground again.

Alan shook his head and marched over. 'No, no, no!' he said, helping Clyde back onto his feet. 'You've got it all wrong. You've got to bend your legs. If you want to ollie you've got to really bend your legs. That's how you get the biggest pop.'

Clyde frowned. 'Okay – and you would know exactly what?'

'As it happens...' Alan's voice trailed off, he took the skateboard from Clyde, and placed a confident foot on it.

Everyone watched as he demonstrated a jump with a perfect, effortless landing.

'King of the concrete. Romford, 1992,' he crowed.

'Yeah, right,' said Clyde, mockingly.

Maria raised her eyes and shook her head. 'Oh no, here we go!'

But Alan wasn't paying any attention. He was

off again across the tarmac – over ramps, up and down, round and round, doing spins, turns and flips, showing off his skills.

He skidded to a graceful halt next to Clyde. 'And he's still got it!' he announced, in a cocky tone.

'But you're old,' mocked Clyde.

'Gotta get pictures of this,' mused Maria, reaching into her bag and pulling out her camera. 'Come on, smile everyone! One... two... three... cheese!'

Sarah Jane, Luke, Clyde and Alan bunched together, arms around one another, beaming proudly into the lens, as Maria snapped off shot after shot, checking her handiwork every so often on the display.

Then her dad took over so that she could be in some of the photographs too. She grinned at the camera, happy to be surrounded by her best mates.

'Let's get one of you on your own, Sarah Jane,' said Maria, after she felt they'd taken enough of the gang.

She ushered her friend to the left, so that the background of the grey and charcoal skate park was replaced with the greens, reds and golds of Ealing Place Park.

'One... two...' Maria lined up a shot of Sarah Jane, placing her in the centre of the frame. But as she stared at the image on the display, the smile suddenly disappeared from her friend's face and she shivered all over. 'What's up?' asked Maria, glancing up.

'Someone just walked over my grave,' said Sarah Jane, and she pulled her cardigan tightly round her. Then she shrugged and smiled once again, but it wasn't as bright a beam this time. 'Come on, quick, take the picture.'

'Smile!' Maria pressed the button.

'Right, let's go home.' Sarah Jane marched off.

Maria put her camera away in her bag and followed her. She couldn't help feeling that the afternoon had ended on a low note, but she wasn't sure why...

In the distance, and half concealed by a leafy sycamore tree, stood a lone figure. But it wasn't a passer-by enjoying a sunny Friday afternoon in the park. This was a tall, sinister shape swathed from head to toe in a hooded, black cloak, with its face completely hidden from view.

And no one saw it. Not even the birds in the trees.

Chapter Two

The silver box

'So why did you give it up?' asked Clyde as he, Luke, Maria, Sarah Jane and Alan turned the corner into Bannerman Road.

'You can't make a living out of a skateboard,' replied Alan.

'That's what Mum said,' Maria pointed out.

'Yeah, well, now she's gone maybe I'll get my board down from the attic.'

'Please say you're joking!'

Alan put his hands on his hips in protest. 'I'm good. Why can't I?'

'Even if you are good, Mr Jackson,' said Clyde, 'you're still too old for a skateboard.' And he let

H 4 T R F G 8 N D 1 S W O B X O 3 T R 2 U F S 7 K

his own board fall to the ground, and he sped off down the road. 'See ya!' he called back, as his silhouette became part of the view.

'Bend your knees!' Alan yelled after him. Then he turned to his daughter. 'Let's get some tea on.'

'I'll just be a minute,' chirped Maria, in her most convincing voice. 'Luke borrowed a textbook and I need it back.'

'I dunno...' sighed her dad, shaking his head. 'What goes on over there?'

'What do you mean?' Maria jumped to her defence a little too quickly. Maybe he'd guessed. 'Nothing goes on over there.'

'I reckon you're having secret parties without me.' Alan chuckled to himself and turned in the direction of number thirty-six.

Maria sighed with relief. He hadn't guessed.

The attic of number thirteen Bannerman Road was a place Maria loved to be. It was full of such fascinating objects, things that would have baffled even the brainiest scientists. She grinned to herself as she looked around.

'Mr Smith, I need you,' called Sarah Jane as she, Luke and Maria faced what, to any normal person, was just a brick chimney breast. But at

Sarah Jane's command, the walls began to open up with great puffs of steam, and from inside emerged a supercomputer, with lights flashing, a bank of futuristic controls and a hi-tech screen.

'Hello, Sarah Jane,' said the computer, in his serious tone.

'Report the position of Meteor K67, please.'

Maria frowned – a meteor? Sarah Jane hadn't mentioned anything about a meteor. What was going on? She didn't like being left out of anything her friend was up to.

Charts, figures and calculations flashed across Mr Smith's display. They went past so quickly that it was almost impossible for Maria to make them out. And even if she could have seen them, they wouldn't have made much sense to her.

'Meteor K67 ascension of twenty hours, thirteen minutes and forty-two seconds. Declination of minus twenty-two degrees. V magnitude brightening from eleven to three point three with a sky motion of eleven point three degrees.'

'It's heading straight for Earth,' explained Luke, turning to Maria. 'And the authorities can't see it because it's coming right through a radar blind spot.'

Maria stared at Luke. 'Of course, why didn't I

H 4 T R F G 8 N D 1 S W O B X O 3 T R 2 U F S 7 K

realise that?' she said, sarcastically. Why had no one mentioned this to her before? There was a meteor hurtling towards Earth!

'If it hits us – bang!' warned Sarah Jane. 'End of the world.'

'You're being a bit calm,' said Maria, baffled as to why they weren't rushing about making plans to stop it.

'Oh, there's no need to worry. When it's in range Mr Smith will create a magnetic pulse and bounce the meteor back out into space. All in a day's work.'

'You're going to save the world and no one will even know about it?'

'I like it better that way,' replied Sarah Jane.

Maria was amazed by her friend's modesty. Some people did the tiniest, most insignificant things and yet boasted about them in the loudest voices. Sarah Jane was the opposite. Without her it was the end for Earth, but she just took it in her stride and never told anyone. As she said, it was all in a day's work for her.

'How long do we have, Mr Smith?' enquired Luke.

'The meteor will be in range of the magnetic pulse at 2.45pm tomorrow.' The computer's lights flashed as he spoke. 'All systems are prepared.'

'You see?' Luke smiled reassuringly at Maria. 'No worries.'

'I know, but I can't help thinking, if it wasn't for Sarah Jane, we'd all be dead!'

'Tell you what, Luke, go put the kettle on. I'm parched.' Sarah Jane smiled at her son. 'Be down in a sec.'

'Sure,' said Luke. 'See you later, Maria.' He left the attic and closed the door behind him.

'Just wanted a word in private,' said Sarah Jane, and she walked over to a set of shelves in the corner of the room lined with books and odd-looking objects.

Maria followed along behind and watched as she ran a finger along the spines of several rows of dusty books. She wondered what her friend wanted with her – the anticipation was exciting, if a little frustrating.

Sarah Jane's hand came to rest on a volume entitled UNIT: Fighting For Humankind. She pulled the book out and put it down on the floor. Then she reached into the space it had left and pulled out a battered brown leather case used to store binoculars.

Maria watched as Sarah Jane opened the case

and produced, not a pair of binoculars, but a much smaller object, wrapped in black velvet. Maria was eager to know what it was.

'This is for you,' Sarah Jane said, unwrapping the velvet to reveal a small silver box, which she proudly handed to Maria.

'Wow!' Maria carefully turned the object around in her hands. The box was perfectly square, about the size of a Rubik's Cube, and etched all over with a strange, ornamental pattern.

'It's beautiful. Where did you get it?'

'Remember that Verron soothsayer we helped fly home the other week? It's from him.'

'But what's it for?' asked Maria, dropping down onto a red chaise longue, still unable to take her eyes off the glittering cube in her hands.

'I don't know,' mused Sarah Jane, sitting down next to her. 'He said, "Remember." Just remember. Whatever that means.'

'So why are you giving it to me?'

'He said, "Give it to the person you trust the most." And that's you. It's probably best not to tell Luke that bit.'

'What's in it?' asked Maria.

'Have a look.'

Maria tried her hardest to slide any of the side

panels, but whichever direction she went in, and however hard she pushed, none of them would yield. The box didn't seem to want to be opened. 'How do you get in?' she asked. 'It's impossible.'

'I tried, too,' admitted Sarah Jane. 'Mr Smith says there's nothing in it. It's just a puzzle box.'

'What's a puzzle box?' asked Maria.

'It's a Japanese thing. They make these ornamental boxes that only the owner can open. And sometimes not even them.'

'Right...'

'I forgot all about it till this afternoon. But there – it's yours.'

'Thank you,' said Maria, smiling warmly at her friend.

'Pop round tomorrow. Let me know how you get on.'

'And we can bash that meteor!'

'Should be fun,' laughed Sarah Jane.

A little after ten o'clock that night, Maria was sat on the edge of her bed in her dressing gown. The only light in the room came from the TV set, which she had turned down low. In her hand was the silver box Sarah Jane had given her earlier. She was determined to open it. It must be possible...

H 4 T R F G 8 N D 1 S W O B X O 3 T R 2 U F S 7 K

She stared at the box for quite some time, turning it around and looking for an obvious opening, a point to get inside. It seemed liked the corners offered the most likely way in, so she twisted them in every direction, pulling as hard as she could on each one in turn.

Then something happened. One of the corners suddenly rotated with a strange crunch, like the sound of tiny cogs grinding against one another.

'Yes!' Maria chirped, triumphantly. 'That must be it!'

Her dad's voice came from downstairs. 'Turn that telly off, Maria! You should be asleep!' It was his strict voice. The one he kept for when he was cross.

'Okay!' Maria called back. However, she didn't do what he'd told her. Instead, she carried on grappling with the box. She knew she was getting close to figuring it out, and was positive something interesting was just about to happen. It was only a matter of finding the correct method. Then the whole thing would spring open and reveal its secret.

But instead, she just hurt her fingers. It was sealed tight. She let out a loud, frustrated grunt.

'Maria!' This time Alan sounded really cross.

Outside, on a darkened Bannerman Road, walked a tall, black-cloaked figure. The same spectre that had haunted the park earlier that day. However, this time it was on a mission. A mission of chaos.

The figure stopped outside number thirteen and turned its hooded gaze upon Sarah Jane's house.

Maria tried one last time to make the box open. It was very late by now and her dad would flip out if he knew she still hadn't gone to sleep.

This time, instead of using all her strength, Maria decided she would twist the box with only the gentlest touch. After all, brute force didn't always get results.

To her surprise something happened. It slid effortlessly open with a diagonal movement, forming two offset pyramid shapes.

She stared at it, grinning, waiting for something amazing to drop out. But nothing did. It just sat there.

'Is that it?' sighed Maria, sad that the box had proved such an anticlimax. She let the alien object fall onto the duvet beside her, then pulled the covers up to her chin and yawned into a much-needed sleep.

H 4 T R F G 8 N D 1 S W O B X O 3 T R 2 U F S 7 K

The black figure raised a slender, pale hand and pointed at Sarah Jane's house. A jewelled ring glinted in the street light.

An eerie rustling noise began, building rapidly from the volume of a hoarse whisper into the clamour of a thunderous storm.

And then, Sarah Jane's car vanished away, leaving only a misty vapour...

Beside Maria, who was now sleeping soundly, the silver box glowed with a strange blue light...

On the street, the menacing figure raised his finger again. This time, all the lights suddenly went off inside number thirteen. And the sound of the wind became the sound of thousands of tiny, urgent voices whispering all at once...

'Dad!' yelled Maria, sitting bolt upright in her bed. And the silver box fell to the floor...

The figure turned away from Sarah Jane's house and, for a moment, the street lights illuminated its face. But there was no face. Just white, featureless skin where the eyes and nose should be, and a twisted, red slash in place of a mouth.

The creature vanished in a whirl of mist...

'What's the matter?' cried Alan, flinging open the door to his daughter's room.

'I'm okay,' replied Maria, out of breath.

'You sure?'

'Yeah, it was just a bad dream.' She tried to smile in order to reassure her dad that everything was fine.

'All right,' said Alan, with a frown of concern, backing out. 'Goodnight.'

After he'd gone, Maria lay still for a few minutes, trying to figure out what had woken her with such a fright. Eventually, exhaustion claimed her, and she drifted off to sleep again.

Beneath her bed, the box, lying forgotten where it had fallen, glowed with a blue light, then slowly faded to darkness.

Chapter Three

The woman at number thirteen

Maria poured milk on her cornflakes, dusted them with a light shower of sugar, and tucked in. She was starving.

'Morning,' Alan said, breezily entering the room. 'You okay now?'

'Yeah,' she replied, through a mouthful of breakfast. 'Fine.'

'Look what I got down from the loft.' Her dad proudly held out his old skateboard.

'Oh, no,' sighed Maria. 'Dad!'

'What? I'm too old, am I?' Alan said, a

little offended.

Maria glanced out of the window. 'Just don't use it anywhere near me...' She trailed off, as something had suddenly caught her eye. But it wasn't outside. It was on the windowsill. 'Where did you get those plants from?'

'Eh?' Her dad looked puzzled. 'From Andrea. Housewarming present. Don't you remember?' He paused. 'That reminds me.' From a drawer he produced an envelope and handed it to Maria. 'You need to sign this. It's her birthday card.'

Maria was confused. 'What do you mean?' she asked, frowning. 'Who's Andrea?'

'Don't be daft. Just sign it.'

'Okay, if you say so.' It must be one of her dad's work friends, thought Maria, though she couldn't recall him mentioning her before. She slid the card out and scribbled her name at the bottom. 'I'm going over the road to see Luke.'

'Luke?' Alan looked up from tinkering with his skateboard. 'Oh, yeah? And Luke's a lad from school, is he?' he asked, in a loaded way.

Maria was baffled. Why was her dad behaving so oddly? 'What's wrong with you this morning?'

As Maria walked up Sarah Jane's drive, she noticed

that her friend's car was missing and in its place was an old, blue banger. Surely she'd not got rid of her cool, green motor in favour of that?

She rang the doorbell and waited.

'Hello, love. You're early.'

Maria couldn't believe her eyes as the door opened. Instead of Sarah Jane, standing in front of her was a total stranger.

'Where's my birthday card then?'

Maria stared at her blankly. What was going on?

'I was only joking,' said the woman, with a reassuring smile.

'Sorry... is Sarah Jane there?' asked Maria, nervously.

'Say again.'

'Sarah Jane.'

'Is that one of your mates from school?'

'No,' said Maria, wondering if this was a relative come to stay. 'Sarah Jane. This is her house.'

'Maria, love, I like a joke, but it's only half-nine in the morning,' said the woman, and she pulled her pale green dressing gown tight around her.

She was about the same age as Sarah Jane, with the same style hair, but hers was auburn, she had a rounder face, and a south London twang to her voice.

'I didn't stop working till gone three,' she continued. 'Once I start painting I can't stop. Try me again a bit later, eh? You can help me get things ready for the party. Sandwiches won't butter themselves.'

'Is Luke there?' Maria asked, eyeing the stranger suspiciously.

'Who?' The woman shook her head and frowned. 'You all right, love?' She paused and stared curiously. 'Maria?'

Maria took a step backwards. This was totally freaking her out. Who was this woman? How did she know her name? Where was her friend? Was she going insane?

Maria burst into the dining room, where her dad was watering the plants with a small copper-coloured can. 'Something really weird is going on,' she began. 'There's this woman in Sarah Jane's house.'

'Sorry?' said Alan, looking up.

'I knocked on the door and there's this other woman stood there.'

'Hold on. What door?'

'Sarah Jane's. Number thirteen,' replied Maria, starting to get frustrated.

'Andrea's?'

'What?'

'Who's Sarah Jane?' Alan put down the watering can and turned to face his daughter.

This was too much for Maria. What was up with everyone today? 'You can stop this right now! It's freaking me out!'

'I'm just not getting you,' said Alan. 'Sarah Jane?'

'Sarah Jane Smith!' cried Maria. 'Our neighbour!'

'There's no one on this road called Sarah Jane. Not that I've met, anyway.'

'Course you have! Stop it! Right – I'll show you!'

Maria opened her laptop and clicked on a folder marked Skate Park. There were twenty or so photo files inside. 'Look!' she declared. 'Sarah Jane is definitely in the photos.'

Alan looked over his daughter's shoulder as she opened the first image.

Maria was horrified by what she saw. She flicked on to the next picture. Then the next. And the next. It was all the same. In every single one, Sarah Jane had been replaced by the woman who'd just answered the door of number thirteen.

It was as if her friend had never existed. But she knew she did exist. Of course she existed. It was everyone else who was going mad, not her. 'Why is she there?' cried Maria. Then she noticed something else. 'Where's Luke?' She stared at her dad, but he just stared straight back at her with an extremely confused expression plastered across his face.

'I'm sorry,' he said, sadly, 'but I don't know any Sarah Janes.' He paused. 'And I don't know any Lukes.'

Maria ignored her dad, stormed from the room, and sat sulkily on the stairs. Pulling her mobile from her pocket, she began scrolling through the phone book. Where had her friend's number gone? It had to be here. This was unbelievable.

Where Sarah Jane's phone number had once been, there was nothing. The list skipped straight from Robbie Chang to School Office. It was as if someone had sneaked in and deleted it without her knowing. But that couldn't possibly have happened. Why would anyone do that?

Next she looked for Luke's number. But that too had disappeared.

And so had Clyde's.

Maria's heart started to beat faster. She couldn't understand it. It was as if part of her life had been erased. Or someone had stolen it.

She tried to recall Clyde's phone number. It was one of those easy ones with lots of zeros and sevens, she was sure. She must be able to remember! 'What is it?' she muttered to herself, frustrated. She thought really hard. 'Of course! That's it!'

Maria dialled the number and pressed the call button.

It was answered after only two rings.

'Who's that?' asked Clyde's voice.

'It's Maria!'

'Who?'

'Me – Maria!'

'Maria Jackson?' Clyde sounded surprised, confused.

'You've got to get over here. Sarah Jane has vanished.'

But he ignored this. 'Maria Jackson from school?'

'Who else would it be?'

'Er... why are you phoning me?' He sounded really puzzled now. 'I didn't give you my number.' A pause. 'Who gave you my number?'

'Clyde, tell me, is Luke with you?'

'Luke?'

'We were out yesterday, skateboarding.'

'I bumped into you at the skate park. No one called Luke though.'

'Luke Smith,' said Maria, urgently. 'Please tell me you're having a joke. Was it Sarah Jane's idea?'

'Who?' asked Clyde.

'Do you know Sarah Jane?'

'Look, if you wanna ask me out, just ask me out.' Clyde laughed. 'I can fit you in next Thursday.'

'But, Clyde, the meteor!' Maria was starting to sweat.

'What meteor?'

'There's a huge meteor heading for Earth!'

'Is there now?'

'Only Sarah Jane can stop it and she's vanished.'

'What are you talking about, you nutter? Laters.' And Clyde hung up.

Maria stood outside Sarah Jane's house and rang the bell. This was getting more and more bizarre by the minute. She had to get to the bottom of it. Perhaps this stranger, Andrea, was holding her friend hostage. Anything seemed possible.

'Hello, love,' said Andrea. 'I've surfaced.' She was now dressed. 'Come on in. Lots to do.'

'Whatever,' said Maria, and she pushed past the

stranger and into the house, determined to find out what was going on.

She flung open the living room door. Instead of Sarah Jane's cluttered yet homely style, with comfortable armchairs and row upon row of scientific books, the room was now light and airy, with a huge TV in the corner, a decorative screen, scatter cushions and the walls covered in modern art.

'But it's... different,' stammered Maria, stunned.

Andrea entered behind her. 'Well, all right, it's a bit of a mess, but I'm going to clean it up before people come round for the party.'

Maria pushed past the woman and ran out of the room. As she did so, the doorbell rang. She ignored it and raced up the two flights of stairs to the attic. She paused outside the room for a moment, dreading what she would find. Then she took a deep breath and shoved open the white, panelled door.

Inside, the attic was a totally different place from the one Maria was used to – just like the living room had been. It was as if Sarah Jane and all the things that made her unique had been shipped out and a whole new life installed there. A much less interesting one.

The scientific equipment, the alien devices, the clutter, the piles of mysterious, nameless objects were all gone. The room was now just a dusty old loft space used to store picture frames and boxes of junk.

Maria stared in disbelief.

Andrea and Alan entered the room.

'Where is she?' demanded Maria.

'I don't know who you're talking about,' replied Andrea.

'Sarah Jane Smith!'

'Never heard of her.'

'Come on, Maria,' said Alan, frowning. 'I think you and I should get back home.'

'But Sarah Jane lives here. In this house. She lives with her son, Luke. Where are they?' Then she remembered something. 'Mr Smith!' She crossed to the wall where the computer lived. A cobweb-covered mirror hung there now. 'I need you!' she called out urgently.

Silence.

Mr Smith was gone too.

'Mr Smith!' wailed Maria again. She was near tears now.

'Sweetheart...' said Alan, softly, placing an arm around his daughter's shoulders. 'There is no Mr

Smith. There's no Sarah Jane. No Smiths at all.'

'But Dad, I...' Maria's voiced faded to silence. She knew there was no point in trying to convince him any more. It was useless. No one believed her.

'We're going home now. Come on.' Alan steered her towards the door.

As they passed Andrea, Maria kept her eyes aimed at the floor. She didn't even want to look at the woman.

'Sorry about this,' said Alan, as they left the room.

Andrea remained rooted to the spot long after her neighbours' footsteps on the stairs had faded to nothing. Then she shivered. It was like someone had walked over her grave.

'Sarah Jane Smith,' she said out loud, for the first time in over forty years.

Chapter Four

The library

M aria was sat in the living room with a cup of tea slowly going cold in her hand. She was resigned to the fact that no one would believe her story. There was no point in going on about it.

Just then, the doorbell rang. She heard her dad's footsteps as he walked down the hall, then the sound of the front door opening.

For one brief moment, Maria let herself believe that maybe the person standing on the other side of the door was Sarah Jane Smith. Perhaps she'd come back. Then she heard a familiar voice and all her hopes vanished. It was her mum. She entered the room, marched over and stood, hands on hips, in front of Maria. Alan hovered in the doorway.

'I've heard your dad's side,' said Chrissie. 'Now

what's going on?'

Maria looked up. 'What are you wearing?' she laughed, as she caught sight of her mum's outfit. It was odd to see her in a supermarket uniform.

'They're my work clothes,' Chrissie said, defensively.

'You've got a job? At the supermarket? But you wouldn't be seen dead working there – wearing that!'

'We've had all this out before,' sighed Chrissie. 'After I dumped Ivan, I needed a bit of extra cash.'

'You dumped Ivan?' Maria was confused. This was the first she'd heard of it.

'How many times do I have to tell you, sweetheart?' Chrissie sounded exasperated. 'After Andrea saw him snogging Lorraine Groom outside the Conservative Club, it was over.' She stared at her daughter, frowning. 'I'm going out with Ricardo now. You've met him plenty of times. Now don't pretend.'

Maria couldn't believe what she was hearing. Today was getting more and more bizarre. Why didn't she remember all these things? They were important. She wouldn't just have forgotten them.

'What's going on, love?' Chrissie sat down on the sofa next to Maria. 'Are you feeling sick? Your dad says you had a bad night.'

'No, Mum, you must remember something! It can't just be me!' pleaded Maria.

But instead of reassuring her, her mum just plastered on a syrupy smile, like a nurse before an operation. 'Tell me about this Sarah Jane girl,' said Chrissie, after a pause.

'She's not a girl, she's an adult!' insisted Maria. 'She's my friend, and Luke's mum. She's a journalist, she always has been. She drives this little green car. And she's funny and clever and brave and she never gives up. You know her, Mum. We all know her.'

'I'm sorry, love, but I don't.'

'And there's something else...' Maria could no longer hold back. She had to explain the danger they were all in. 'Something's going to happen today. Something terrible. And only Sarah Jane can stop it.'

'And what's that then?' asked Alan, coming over and perching on the arm of the sofa.

'There's a meteor!' Maria blurted out. 'It's going to destroy the world! Unless Sarah Jane can get rid of it!'

Later, Alan and Chrissie sat on opposite sides of the kitchen table. There was a long silence broken only

H 4 T R F G 8 N D 1 S W O B X O 3 T R 2 U F S 7 K

by a bird chirping in the back garden.

'You know what this is? A cry for attention,' said Chrissie at last. 'She's had all these disruptions. She's been bottling it up. And now it is all coming out. I knew it would happen. I was just waiting.'

'So, this Sarah Jane – she's just dreamt her up?'

'Imaginary friend. And this Luke she keeps talking about, he's like the brother she never had.'

'What does that make Sarah Jane?' asked Alan, frowning at his ex-wife. 'The mother she never had?'

'Oh, that's right,' Chrissie snapped, narrowing her eyes. 'Have a pop at me. Here we go. Make it all about Alan and what Alan thinks.' She got up out of the seat, grabbed her handbag from the table and headed for the door. 'I'm not listening to this.'

'Maria is in pieces!' called Alan, angrily.

'Then you put them back together again!' hissed Chrissie. 'If your theory's correct she won't want her real, terrible mother hanging about, will she?' Chrissie stomped out of the room and, a few seconds later, the front door slammed shut.

Maria sat on the edge of her bed with her laptop open in front of her. Alan sat next to her, holding the family photo album.

'Okay, so yesterday evening, what did we do?'

'I picked you up from school,' said her dad. 'Then we went to the park.'

'We went with Andrea?' asked Maria.

'No. She was just passing by. We also bumped into a lad you know from school – Clyde.'

'Who I don't really know,' said Maria, sadly, remembering the phone call from earlier.

'You said you knew him vaguely. He's in some of your classes.'

'And you showed off your skateboarding to him?' enquired Maria, seeing if their versions of yesterday matched up at all.

'That's right. And you were cringing. Thanks,' Alan added, sarcastically.

Maria thought for a moment. 'So when did I first meet Andrea?'

Alan opened the photo album and turned a few pages in. 'That's us outside,' he said, kindly. 'The day we moved in. Andrea came over and gave us a hand.'

Maria stared at the photo which showed her and her dad carrying boxes into the house, and Andrea helping them. 'But Sarah Jane was there. That's when we met her. She was all frosty. You've got to remember that.'

Alan shook his head. 'Just Andrea. And she was lovely. Invited us over straight away. She's always having parties,' he said, turning to the next page. 'She lives life to the full does Andrea.'

Maria looked at the pictures of a party at number thirteen she didn't recall going to. But there she was with this Andrea person and her dad, looking as if she was having a fantastic time. But how was that possible? She didn't remember anything about it. Who took the picture? What were they celebrating? 'I don't remember any of that,' she said, sadly.

'Perhaps you should get some sleep.' Alan looked concerned. 'Nice little nap, then maybe you'll feel better.'

'You want me to forget Sarah Jane.'

'There is no Sarah Jane.'

'But she was so real to me. All the things we did, the incredible things we saw...' Maria remembered the look on her friend's face whenever they defeated an alien menace. So jubilant, so proud of herself, and of Maria. She couldn't have made up an amazing look like that, surely?

'Something happened last night and Sarah Jane vanished,' she said, determinedly. 'Nobody remembers. But I do. And somehow when everything changed, I got protected. I'm telling you,

Dad, I'm right. And I'm gonna show you!'

Maria double-clicked on the Internet icon on her computer desktop. A window sprung open. In the search engine she typed the words Sarah Jane Smith and hit the return key.

'Sarah Jane Smith – solicitors,' she read from the list. 'Sarah Jane Smith – Guernsey Women's Football.' Maria scratched her head and scrolled down. 'There must be some reference...'

'I don't think there will be.'

'Hang on.' Something had caught her eye. 'My Poems by Carla Morgan. For Sarah Jane Smith,' she read, and then clicked on the link. 'For Sarah Jane Smith, who left us on 12th July 1964.' Maria turned to look at her dad. 'The woman who wrote this, she's the same age as Sarah Jane.'

'So?' said Alan, dismissively.

'1964... have they got newspapers in the library? Old newspapers?'

'They should have.' Alan looked puzzled.

'Come on then!' grinned Maria, leaping up. 'Off to the library!'

'Schoolgirl Sarah Jane Smith, thirteen,' read Maria, 'died yesterday after falling from Westport Pier in a tragic accident...'

Maria and Alan were at one of the computers that held the library's newspaper archive.

'It's just the same name, darling,' said Alan.

She grinned, pleased with herself at having found some mention of her friend. Even if it only spelt tragedy, at least Sarah Jane had existed.

Maria continued to read. 'A second girl, Andrea Yates, is being treated for shock...' She glanced up at her dad. He no longer had that worried look on his face, as if he thought Maria was going mad. He appeared concerned in a different way now.

'But that's our Andrea from the across the road,' he said, sounding puzzled. 'She's Andrea Yates.'

'You see – I'm not lying. There's a connection.'

Alan frowned. 'Did Andrea tell you about this accident? Is that where you've got the name from?'

'Why would I do that?' she protested. 'I'm telling the truth!'

Just then something very peculiar happened. As Maria stared at the article on the screen, the names Sarah Jane Smith and Andrea Yates changed places. She could hardly believe her eyes. 'Look!' She elbowed her dad. 'The names have swapped over.' But in the blink of an eye, the page was once more as it had been. Alan had missed it.

'No, they haven't,' he said.

Then something else peculiar happened. Maria was sure she heard Sarah Jane's voice quietly calling her name. 'Maria...' it seemed to whisper. But it wasn't like someone standing in the room with you. It was like an echo of an echo transported on the breeze from dozens of miles away.

'That's Sarah Jane's voice!' cried Maria, excitedly. 'It's her voice! I'm sure it is!'

'You can hear voices now?'

'Dad, it was her!'

'You need to calm down,' said Alan.

They were being glared at by a grumpy-looking librarian.

'But you've seen the evidence,' said Maria, more quietly.

'There is no evidence.'

'But I've worked it out,' she hissed. 'Andrea's done something and Sarah Jane's gone. Just as that meteor is about to smash into us.'

'That's enough!' said Alan, sounding quite cross this time. 'I think we should take you to see a doctor!'

'Maybe Andrea did say something about the accident,' said Maria, as she and Alan left the library and turned out onto the main road.

She knew there was no way her dad was ever going to believe her, and the last thing she wanted was to find herself on a psychiatrist's couch. She wasn't mad. She knew she wasn't. But convincing other people was going to be tough. It was best, for the time being, to keep her theories to herself.

'Well, that must be it,' said Alan, with relief.

'And that nightmare – perhaps I've got it all mixed up. I'm really sorry.' Maria paused and looked her dad in the eye. 'Of course I know Andrea,' she lied.

Alan smiled and hugged his daughter tightly. 'I've been so worried,' he said.

'I didn't hear a voice,' added Maria, knowing she had to be as convincing as possible. 'I was just making that up.'

'But why, sweetheart?'

'I dunno,' she shrugged. 'I think I just wanted some attention.'

'Is there something else wrong?' Alan frowned. 'Something at school?' He paused, suddenly looking uneasy. 'Have I done something wrong?'

'No,' said Maria, shaking her head. 'It's just me.'

'If there's anything you want to talk about, I'll give you all the attention in the world.'

'Thanks, Dad.'

They walked on for a few moments in silence.

Maria knew she had to find out the truth about the day Sarah Jane supposedly died falling off that pier, but she had to be careful. She didn't want her dad to suspect a thing.

'Perhaps I should go and see Andrea,' she ventured, trying to sound innocent. 'I ought to go and say sorry.'

Alan nodded. 'Good idea.'

'Oh, that's all right, love,' said Andrea in a sympathetic tone. 'There's no need to apologise. I remember when I was your age...' She smiled to herself. 'The thoughts that would come into my head sometimes.'

'I don't know where I got that name – Sarah Jane Smith.' Maria was carefully testing the water. She wondered whether the mention of her friend would get any kind of reaction.

'Means nothing to me, love,' replied Andrea, coolly.

'Positive?' asked Maria.

'Positive.'

Maria scanned the impostor's face, but there was nothing. Not even a flicker of recognition, or a hint of guilt.

'But how could you forget?' asked Maria, a hard

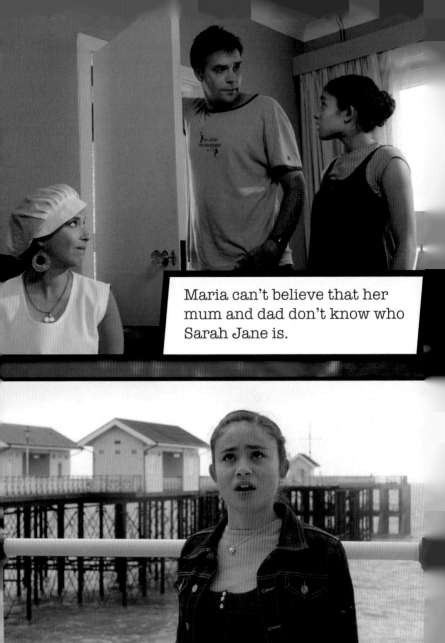

Maria can't believe that her mum and dad don't know who Sarah Jane is.

Maria finds herself standing in a strange seaside town.

'Pleased to meet you,' the girl said with a smile. 'I'm Sarah Jane Smith.'

The date at the top of the newspaper reads 12th July 1964!

'Please, Clyde,' cried Alan. 'You must remember my daughter, Maria!'

The young Sarah Jane tells Andrea not to go on to the pier.

'Andrea, grab my hand!' Sarah Jane shouts at her friend.

Suddenly it is Sarah Jane that is dangling from the pier.

A tall faceless figure in a black cloak gives Andrea a silver box.

The Graske tries to wriggle free of the ropes that Alan has tied him up in.

Alan presses a button on the strange alien-looking device.

Alan is so relieved that Maria is back. He hugs her tightly.

The Graske finally escapes from the ropes and teleports away.

note suddenly entering her voice. She wasn't going to let Andrea off the hook that easily. '1964... school trip... the pier...' She stared into the woman's eyes. 'She fell. She died. And you were with her.'

'What?!' exclaimed Andrea, her face turning suddenly pale.

So she did remember, thought Maria. She knew it! 'You lived and she died. Only that wasn't meant to happen. The key moment, when everything in the world changed...'

Maria watched as Andrea's eyes became empty, sad. It was as if she'd left the room, left Bannerman Road, and was back in 1964, remembering the terrible events of that day on the pier. She looked haunted – pale and haunted by the past.

Then no sooner had she drifted away than she was back again, her expression now full of rage. She turned her angry glare upon Maria. 'Get out of my house!' she snapped.

'This isn't your house!' Maria snapped back. 'This is some kind of time gone wrong. Because in my world, the way things should've been, you died!'

'Get out!' shouted Andrea, pushing Maria away from her and towards the door. 'I've had enough of this! I'm phoning your dad! Get out!'

Maria backed out into the hall, Andrea advancing

on her all the while. 'Just to let you know – I'm going to sort things out.' She was now flat against the front door. 'I'm going to work out how time got changed, find Sarah Jane, and then I'm going to bring her back!' Maria took a deep breath. 'And nothing is going to stop me!'

Chapter Five

The attic mirror

'No!' moaned Andrea to herself. 'Oh, no!' And she ran up the stairs and into the attic. 'That day.... the pier...' She looked around the dusty, cobweb-filled room. There was something she knew she had to find. Something she hadn't seen in decades. But where was it? What was it? She couldn't even remember.

Andrea searched through a crate filled with old crockery and saucepans she didn't use any more. Nothing. Then she looked in another, but this only held books she'd read long ago and forgotten. She turned over another packed with bank statements, bills and letters from friends she hadn't seen in years.

Finally, digging deep in a cracked tea chest with rusty binding shoved into a dark corner, beneath stacks of yellowed newspapers and an out-of-fashion cocktail dress, she found something. The something she was looking for.

'Oh, Sarah...'

Wrapped in a satin scarf was a silver box. It was etched all over with a strange, ornamental pattern.

As she stared at the box, she heard a low, sinister voice. 'Remember...' it called, drawing out every syllable. 'Andrea... remember...'

But where was it coming from? No, it couldn't be!

Still holding the box, Andrea slowly walked towards the mirror. She stared into the dusty glass, in which suddenly there appeared the shape of a black-cloaked figure. Andrea span around, but there was no one standing behind her. He seemed only to exist in the mirror.

But instead of screaming or running out of the room like any normal person would do, Andrea found herself strangely calm. This shape, this being, was more familiar to her than she at first realised.

'Who are you?' she demanded, terrified.

'Remember!' he said, in the same hushed echo.

'Remember!'

And that was when it all came back to her. Everything that had happened when she was thirteen; on that school trip to Westport. It was as if it had taken place this morning, it was so sharp in her mind's eye.

'I forgot you,' she said, stunned at her poor memory. 'I forgot what I did that day. All these years, living this life...'

'You forgot me, Andrea Yates. But I never forgot you.'

Andrea shuddered.

'The day she died, you gave me this.' She stared at the box in her hand.

'My gift,' said the faceless figure. 'But why are you calling me now?'

'Maria Jackson, over the road,' said Andrea. 'All of a sudden, she keeps going on about Sarah Jane. She knows. She knows what I did that day – and she's made me remember.' It was so painful for her to recall.

'She's just a child. Nobody will listen.'

'But I can't bear it...' She looked down once again at the box. 'How could I forget what I did, what we agreed? Did you make me forget?'

'Your life is better, is it not?'

'Yes,' Andrea admitted, after a pause, and she nodded her head sadly. The tears were starting to force their way out the corners of her eyes. She strained to hold them back.

'What do you want from me?' asked the creature, its tiny, sharpened teeth glinting in the half-light of the attic.

'Change her back the way she was – the girl over the road. Make her forget.'

'I can't. There is a barrier. She is protected, somehow.' He paused. 'But I can remove her for you.'

'No!' cried Andrea. 'Not killing!'

'I cannot kill,' he replied. 'But I can stop her ruining your life. One night's sleep and you will forget her, forget me, forget everything, once more.'

'Remove her where?'

'This need not concern you. But I need your agreement. Do I have it?'

Andrea struggled with herself. She knew it was wrong, yet what could she do? If she was to continue living this life, then she must agree to what this meddler in time suggested. 'Yes,' she said, forcing the word out. A tear trickled down her cheek.

'It shall be arranged. But first, Andrea Yates,

you must separate the child from her father...'

Maria now knew she was right. It was Andrea who should have died falling off Westport Pier when she was thirteen years old. Someone, something, had got in the way and now everything was the opposite of what it ought to be.

And it seemed that Maria was the only one in the entire world who knew that time had been turned on its head. Everyone else believed this was the way things had always been. They thought that this was how life was meant to turn out – for better or worse. Maria knew the truth. But what could she do about it? Without Sarah Jane she was lost.

She sat on the edge of her bed hugging her knees. It was then that she heard a disembodied voice.

'Maria... help me...' it called.

It was Sarah Jane. But where was she?

Maria leapt up and scanned the room, but her friend was nowhere to be seen. Then she saw her. She was in the mirror.

Sarah Jane looked lost and afraid. She couldn't see Maria.

'What can I do?' cried Maria, into the glass. 'Where do I start? The meteor, I can't do anything to stop it... why is it only me who remembers you?'

'Maria... please...'

Maria checked over her shoulder to see if Sarah Jane was in the room with her, but she wasn't. It was unbelievable how she could see her only in the mirror. However, by the time she turned back, her friend was gone, and Maria was alone.

She threw herself down on the bed, sad and dejected. She'd been so close to making contact with Sarah Jane, and if she could have made contact, then she could have proved to everyone she wasn't crazy after all. But it was too late.

Maria let out a long, weary sigh. Maybe she was going mad.

But just then her foot brushed against something under her bed. It was the silver box that her friend had given her yesterday. She'd completely forgotten about it until now.

Maria picked it up and turned it around in her hand. Her face lit up. For the first time in ages she felt there was hope again.

'Yes!' she called out, triumphantly. 'I've been so thick!'.

'You sure you don't mind giving me a hand?'

'Not at all,' replied Alan, as he followed Andrea

across the road to number thirteen.

'I've got this banner, for my birthday party, and I want to put it up over the front door. I need another pair of hands.'

Andrea went inside the house and brought out a chair for Alan to stand on. Then she handed him the banner with Happy Birthday emblazoned on it, and he climbed up so he was at eye level with the doorframe, and he started to secure it firmly in place.

'I've never really gone big on birthdays myself,' he said, keeping his eyes fixed on his task. 'I don't like being the centre of attention really. I used to when I was a kid. I had big birthday parties then, of course...'

Alan continued to chatter on, but Andrea wasn't listening any more. She was staring across the road at number thirty-six, where Maria was now all alone...

'Dad, I've worked it out!' crowed Maria, proudly, as she skipped down the stairs and into the hallway. 'It's this box – it protected me...' She trailed off.

Alan wasn't there any more. And the house was eerily quiet. What's more, Maria had a feeling that something bad was just about to happen.

'Dad?' she called again, freezing at the bottom of the stairs.

All at once, there was a blinding bright flash of blue light, and a strange vortex formed in front of her. In the middle of it, out of thin air, there appeared a hideous alien creature, the like of which Maria had never seen before.

No taller than a small child, it had stumpy legs and stubby arms. Its face resembled a goblin, with three tusk-like spikes sprouting from its mottled, bald head. It had sharp, vicious teeth, a pointed chin and beady, staring eyes.

The monster growled menacingly at Maria and she let out a scream. Before she had time to make a run for it, it had pointed a strange alien gun at her.

Thinking fast, Maria ducked. Two wires zoomed from the gun's muzzle and whizzed over her head. But as she dropped to the floor, the silver box fell out of her hand.

Before the creature had a chance to fire again, she rushed down the hallway and into the kitchen. She fumbled with the key to the backdoor. She had to get out of the house. Turn, for goodness sake, she thought. Luckily, the key soon swivelled round, the door opened, and she dashed outside into the back garden.

But she'd lost valuable seconds and the alien was hot on her heels...

Maria raced down the side of the house, along Bannerman Road and around the corner. From the snarling noise she could hear behind her, she knew the monster was close. And when she glanced back over her shoulder, she could see its dumpy little legs pounding up and down. He was gaining on her.

She had now reached the edge of the local recreation ground, and she raced across the grass, hoping the uneven surface would slow the creature down.

But it didn't.

Maria ran as fast as she could. Faster than she'd ever managed during games at school. Then she had an idea, and took a sharp left into an archway beneath the railway bridge. She hoped this would shake off the alien. But she'd never taken this exit from the park before, and was horrified by what greeted her.

It wasn't an exit at all. She'd landed herself with a dead end. The archway led only to a high metal fence with no way through. She was trapped.

She span around and, just as she feared, the hideous alien was advancing on her from behind, closing in, with his gun pointing squarely at her.

What could she do? Nothing!

Sarah Jane had taught her to always look her enemy in the eye – and that's just what she did. If nothing else, she was going to go out with dignity. And even in that most terrifying moment, she still found the strength to smile. Perhaps it was the ridiculousness of the situation. Or maybe it was how daft the little alien looked.

Maria held her breath.

The creature let out a cackle and fired its weapon. Two wires sprang out and attached themselves to Maria's jacket. Then, in the blink of an eye, both she and the alien had become nothing more than a whirl of vapour. And then that too had disappeared.

Chapter Six

The
time slip

Alan was standing in the hallway of number thirty-six Bannerman Road. 'Maria?' he called. 'Are you okay?' Silence. 'Maria?' Then his foot stubbed against something. He looked down at the floor. There was a silver box lying there. He picked it up and examined it closely.

It was like nothing he'd ever seen before. It looked bizarre. So strange, in fact, it could have come from another world. 'Maria?' he called again, but there was no reply.

He turned his attentions back to the shiny object in his hand. What could it be for, he wondered, and how did it get into the house?

Suddenly, it began to glow with a peculiar blue light. The light flickered across Alan's face and, as it did so, he lost his balance and staggered backwards. The room faded in and out of focus, everything was spinning, losing its distinction and blurring into one confused mass. The sounds Alan heard were distorted and strained. He felt sick inside. What was going on?

If he'd been able to concentrate, Alan would have seen all the photographs of his daughter on display in the room, suddenly vanish. The ones on the sideboard, on the mantelpiece and on the windowsill all evaporated into thin air.

It was as if Maria had never existed.

'Alan?' called a distant voice. 'Alan!'

He sank to his knees, terrified, woozy.

And then the storm in his head subsided, and everything suddenly seemed even calmer than it had before.

'The backdoor was wide open.' It was Chrissie. 'You wanna be careful.'

'What was that?' asked Alan, still dazed and spinning from the avalanche in his head.

'What was what?' Chrissie looked confused. 'Come on, let's go over to Andrea's.'

'And what about Maria?' Alan wondered where

his daughter had got to.

'Who?' she asked. 'Don't say you've finally got yourself a new woman.'

'Maria was in here. I think she's run off.'

'What, already? Sensible woman, whoever she is. It took me fourteen years.'

Alan couldn't understand what she meant. 'I mean Maria. Our Maria.'

Chrissie frowned. 'What do you mean – ours?'

'Our daughter!' insisted Alan, starting to get frustrated. What was the matter with the woman today?

'Oh, Alan, don't start messing about. I know you wanted kids, but I never did. As if I've got a maternal bone in my body!'

'Chrissie, stop this now!' He was really exasperated. Why was she being so contrary? 'Maria is our daughter!'

'There is no Maria. Maria doesn't exist!'

Alan couldn't believe what he was hearing. This was madness.

Maria looked around her, blinking. She was on a strange, stony pathway suspended in midair, with nothing holding it up. Where was this place, she wondered?

In front of her was the creature with three tusks, and he was towing Maria along behind him using the two lengths of wire that were still attached to her jacket.

'Where are you taking me?' Maria demanded.

The little alien did not reply, but she knew that wherever it was, it wouldn't be pleasant.

She had to escape.

Summoning all her strength, both physical and mental, she yanked violently at the wires that held her. They snapped off with an echoing clack and immediately her body started to tingle all over. Her captor and the rocky pathway disappeared, and she felt herself falling, falling, falling through space. Her stomach leapt up into her mouth, leaving her breathless and frightened.

The next thing she knew she was hitting the ground, like she'd tripped over, or had woken too quickly from a dream.

Maria lay motionless for a second or two, checking to see if she'd broken anything in the fall. Surprisingly, she was fine.

She slowly hoisted herself up, dusted off her clothes, and looked cautiously around. 'Where am I?' she murmured, under her breath.

She was standing on the concrete promenade of

a seaside town. But which seaside town? There was a long pier stretching out to sea. There were people on the beach and swimming in the water. Others were wandering up and down the promenade. Kids ran about holding huge clouds of pink candyfloss, while elderly men sat and read newspapers under knotted handkerchief hats.

But there was something weird about it all, she thought. Something wasn't right. Maria had been to the seaside plenty of times, but it had been nothing like this.

A young couple walked by listening to music. But instead of having their mobiles turned up, they were carrying a massive, old-fashioned radio – the type you see in junk shops. And the song playing was from years ago. What's more, their clothes were all wrong. Like something out of a dull, Sunday afternoon film. The cars, too, were out of date, and so were the bicycles... and the hand-pulled cart of an ice-cream seller. Where was she?

Two teenage girls walked past wearing matching bright yellow summer school dresses and brown cardigans.

'Come on, it'll be a laugh,' one said to the other. 'Better than that crummy museum.'

'But it's dangerous,' replied her friend.

Maria had to speak to someone, find out where she was and what was going on. She walked up to the schoolgirls and stopped them mid-conversation. 'Excuse me,' she said, awkwardly. 'I'm going to sound mad... but where is this?'

The one with red hair looked Maria up and down, disapprovingly. 'You've got a nerve, going out dressed like that. Look at her!' And she nudged her companion and giggled.

'Don't be so rude,' chided her brown-haired friend. 'Are you all right? You look a bit lost.'

'I think I am,' said Maria. 'I was in London... I'm Maria Jackson.'

The brown-haired girl held out her hand. 'Pleased to meet you,' she said with a smile. 'I'm Sarah Jane Smith.'

As Maria took the outstretched hand, she realised the truth. It was almost unbelievable, totally impossible, but it had happened. She had gone back in time to 1964. And this was Sarah Jane when she was young.

If it hadn't been for the fact that she'd left her own time under deadly threat from a meteor, she would have relished the chance to visit the past and find out what life was like back then. Back now. However, things were too serious for her to take a holiday.

'Hello, Sarah Jane Smith,' she grinned. It was impossible not to grin. There she was, all those years ago, pretty much the same age as Maria was now. And she had that old familiar expression, the one Maria knew so well – serious yet reassuring. And the same inscrutable eyes. Even her hairstyle hadn't really changed.

Sarah Jane smiled back.

Maria turned to the other girl. 'And you're Andrea Yates?' she asked.

'So what if I am?' she replied, sulkily. 'I don't know you. How come you know my name?'

Maria bit her lip. Even if she did try to explain how she knew, the girl would never believe her. After all, it was a ridiculous idea – to have travelled back in time. Maybe she was dreaming it. Or perhaps it was all a trick. A sinister, staged illusion. She needed to make sure this really was the past, so she looked around her for evidence. Lying on the ice-cream seller's cart was a newspaper. She scooted over and glanced at the front page. The date at the top read: 12th July 1964. So it was true.

'I've gone back in time!' She couldn't help saying it out loud. This was so remarkable. 'Sarah Jane, I will know you.'

'She's a loony!' laughed Andrea. 'Come on, leave her alone. Those people don't know their own strength.'

'Don't be so mean,' said Sarah Jane, frowning at her friend. She turned back to Maria. 'If you're lost, I'll take you to our teacher.'

'We're not going back – it's boring,' sighed Andrea.

'And you're going down the pier?' asked a panicked Maria. 'Right now?' This was the very day the accident happened that led to one of the girls dying. She had to do something to stop them.

'It's closed off,' said Andrea.

Good job too, thought Maria.

'But we'll get through,' continued the redhead, defiantly. 'I want to explore.'

'But you mustn't!' cried Maria. 'Sarah Jane, you've got to believe me! You mustn't go down there!'

'Why not?' asked Sarah Jane, looking confused.

'It's today, the accident.' She was frightened now, worried for her friend's life. 'It's about to happen. Look, I shouldn't be here, but I was travelling with this... thing...' She was speaking more and more quickly. 'It's too complicated to explain, but I broke free, and I must have ended up here because this was the last place he came to. Because he was here

– in 1964. He must've been. He swapped you two.'

'Hang on,' said Sarah Jane, shaking her head. 'I'm not getting any of this.'

'There's nothing to get,' interrupted Andrea. 'She's creepy.' And she grabbed hold of Sarah Jane's arm.

'Just listen to me!' insisted Maria, in a high-pitched voice. 'It's not safe! Go back, both of you, find your mates! Just get back on the coach to school! Go home!'

'I told you she was mad,' said Andrea, tugging roughly at her friend. 'Come on, leave her!' And she pulled Sarah Jane away.

Maria stood alone, watching the girls as they walked off towards the pier. There was nothing she could do to stop them, short of physically restraining them. But that would only cause a scene and would get her nowhere.

Just then there was a flash of light and the pint-sized alien appeared on the promenade. The second Maria caught sight of him she turned to run, but she wasn't quick enough, and she felt the impact of the two wires as they once again gripped onto her jacket. Then the hold on her tightened and she was whizzing through the blankness of time. Oh, no. Not again, thought Maria.

Standing at the sealed-up entrance to the pier, emblazoned with an authoritative NO ENTRY sign painted in red, the young Sarah Jane glanced back for a final look at the strange girl wearing strange clothes.

But she was nowhere to be seen.

'Where did she go?' she asked Andrea.

'Who cares?' said her friend, without looking round. She rattled the iron gates that separated her from the pier. 'What a creep!'

'She said we shouldn't – '

'Don't be so dull!'

'But she was scared. It's weird. I sort of believed her.'

'You'd believe a Triffid was going to come and get us if someone told you it was.'

Sarah Jane watched as Andrea heaved one of the gates open a crack, and discreetly slipped through.

'Just follow me – I'll look after you,' said Andrea.

Sarah Jane glanced around her guiltily. Then she squeezed through the gap and onto the deserted pier.

Chapter Seven

The land of limbo

Maria found herself lying at the tusked creature's feet. He disconnected the wires that held them together and immediately teleported off.

She was now alone – or at least she assumed she was – in a completely white field. Or was it a field? It wasn't really anything. It was just a vast, endless quantity of nothing. Like a room the size of forever, thought Maria, without walls, without a ceiling, without a floor. She could see for as far as it was possible, yet there was nothing in sight.

'Where is this?' she asked herself out loud, starting to get scared.

'You tell me,' came a voice.

'Sarah Jane!' Maria span round, and there, standing right behind her, was her friend. They ran into one another's arms and hugged for a long time.

'I thought I'd never see you again,' stammered Maria, so relieved to be with Sarah Jane again. So she hadn't imagined her after all. 'It's so good to see you.'

'It's good to see you, too. I was all on my own.'

Maria pulled away and looked around her. 'Where are we?' she asked. 'Is this a different planet?'

'I don't think we're anywhere at all. We're in limbo.'

'What does that mean?'

'It's nowhere, it's nothing,' said Sarah Jane, sadly. 'We're lost.'

Back in the present day, at number thirty-six Bannerman Road, Alan stared into his ex-wife's eyes. He couldn't believe she was behaving so oddly – pretending Maria didn't exist. 'But you came here earlier to see her,' he appealed. 'It's our own daughter, Chrissie, she's disappeared!'

'This isn't funny, Alan. We never had any kids.'

'But she's about that high.' He indicated how tall

Maria was. 'She's got dark hair, like me, and she's beautiful.'

'Are you getting some sort of kick out of this?' asked Chrissie, forcefully. 'There is no Maria! This is cruel! Now stop it!' She paused. 'Maybe if there had been,' she said, with a note of what sounded to Alan like regret, 'we wouldn't have split up. But it's too late for that now.'

Alan realised he was never going to get through to her. She really believed that their daughter didn't exist. But what had happened? Why wouldn't she acknowledge Maria's existence? He looked down at the silver box, which he still held tightly in his sweaty hand. Then suddenly, like a light being turned on in the darkness, the truth hit him. 'It's this box!' he announced, triumphantly.

'Oh, you're full of nonsense, you are,' sighed Chrissie. 'Right, I'm going to Andrea's birthday party. Are you coming or not? Although, as she's real flesh and blood, she's probably not your type.'

But Alan wasn't listening. He was already rushing out of the room, up the stairs and into Maria's bedroom. What greeted him there didn't surprise him at all.

The room that only minutes before had been his daughter's, now lay virtually empty. It was merely a storage space, occupied by the odds and ends that didn't fit into the other rooms. No bed, no desk, no curtains, no wardrobe filled with brightly coloured clothes. No trace of Maria at all. It was as if she had never existed.

'You should make this into a utility room,' said Chrissie, entering and glancing about. 'I know I keep saying that but – '

'This was her bedroom,' interrupted Alan.

'Stop it!'

'She said she was protected. Something protected her.' Alan held up the box, studying it carefully from every angle. 'What if this protected her?'

'If we've got a daughter then where is she? Look!' said Chrissie, picking up a photo album that was lying on top of a box. She flicked through it, stopped on a particular page, and held it out so Alan could see. 'This is the day you moved in. Andrea came to help. I took the photo. You and her, and me. No one called Maria.'

Alan stared in disbelief at the photograph. It was the same one he'd showed his daughter earlier that day to prove Andrea existed. However, this time, there was only himself and Andrea moving boxes – no Maria.

'Maria was telling the truth,' he accidentally said

out loud. All the time she'd claimed not to remember Andrea – perhaps she wasn't crazy. Maybe to Maria she didn't exist.

'This is why we broke up!' snorted Chrissie. 'People used to say, "But he's gorgeous – why didn't it work out?" Well, this just brings it all flooding back.'

But Alan wasn't listening. He was thinking back over everything his daughter had said. 'What if there's meant to be a Maria? And someone else... a woman called Sarah Jane Smith...'

In the land of limbo, Maria watched Sarah Jane's face fill with sadness as she recalled what had happened all those years ago.

'Andrea Yates... oh, I could never forget.' Her friend took a long, weary breath. 'When I was thirteen, we were on a school trip. We went onto the pier. She fell and there was nothing I could do.' She paused 'I always thought – that could have been me...'

'But she's alive,' explained Maria. 'It's like she's always been alive.'

'Really?' Sarah Jane's eyes widened. 'What sort of woman is she?'

'Bit full-on, likes to party,' replied Maria.

Sarah Jane smiled. 'That sounds like Andrea.' She paused. 'And what was I like – when I was a teenager?'

'It was weird,' admitted Maria. 'Although you looked so different, I knew deep down that it was the same person. Something about your eyes and the way you moved your mouth and held your arms. It was bizarre.'

'I was such a timid little thing back then,' said Sarah Jane, with a wistful sigh. 'Andrea was always bossing me about, and I ended up following her. I didn't really know what I wanted from life. I knew I had to do something important, something that mattered, I just didn't know what.' She threw her head back and closed her eyes for a moment. 'It was only when I met the Doctor that the pieces of the jigsaw finally slotted into place. He was so amazing, I wanted to follow in his footsteps.'

'And you did,' Maria reassured her. 'You've done amazing things – just like him.' She smiled at her friend. 'You're my Doctor.'

Sarah Jane put her arms around Maria and pulled her into a tight embrace. 'I'm not anyone's anything,' she said, sadly, after finally breaking away. 'I don't even exist any more.'

'So, in the parallel world, you died, and she lived?'

'It's not a parallel world. If only. It's our timeline, and it's been changed.'

Maria was finding it hard to grasp. She'd thought this was merely another version of events running alongside reality. But it seemed these strange new happenings had actually replaced reality. 'But without you that meteor must still be on its way.' Maria started to panic. 'It's going to smash into Earth!'

'And if I'm not there, that means the end of the world.'

Maria stared at Sarah Jane, terrified at the thought of what might be happening on Earth at any moment. But how could they get back there and stop it?

'I was the only one that knew about the changes,' she said. 'I got protected, somehow, by that box.'

'The box – of course!' Sarah Jane smiled. 'The Verron soothsayer must have known this was going to happen. Do you remember what I told you he said? "Give it to the person you trust the most." It linked us somehow. I could sense you searching for me. I called out to you.'

'But I dropped it. I lost it,' admitted Maria, guiltily. 'That little alien thing came along and I ran.' She paused. 'Did he do all this?'

'No,' said Sarah Jane, shaking her head. 'That alien, he's called a Graske. There was some Graske activity on Earth a couple of years back, but this isn't their style at all.'

'What do you mean?' Maria asked, confused.

'This is much more powerful. Some other creature must be using the Graske – as a slave.'

'Sarah Jane...' A sinister, disembodied voice filled the air.

'Who's that?' Maria span round to see who it was, but there was no one there.

The voice called her friend again.

'I'm being summoned,' said Sarah Jane, ominously. 'Maria, you stay here.'

'Don't leave me on my own!' It was bad enough being trapped in this endless whiteness, this nothingness, but being without Sarah Jane sent shivers down Maria's spine.

'Oh, I'll come back, I promise. I'll never leave you, Maria. Never. Have you got that?' She hugged Maria reassuringly. 'Just wait.'

'Okay,' nodded Maria. 'I'll wait.' She tried to sound brave, but inside she was terrified at the thought of being left all alone in this vast, empty wasteland at the edges of Time.

'Sarah Jane...' the voice called again.

Maria watched sadly as her friend walked off into the distance, then disappeared completely, blotted out by the whiteness.

Chapter Eight

The birthday party

Outside number thirteen Bannerman Road, Andrea stood welcoming the guests as they arrived for her birthday party. Her hair was beautifully styled, her face was made-up and she wore an elegant black outfit. In one hand she held a glass of champagne.

'Thank you so much for coming,' she cooed to a guest, and kissed her warmly on both cheeks.

'Thank you for inviting us,' smiled the woman, and headed inside the house.

'It wouldn't be the same without you,' Andrea

called after her. 'Go and find yourself a drink.'

An elderly couple approached.

'Hello, Joan,' said Andrea, to the woman. 'How are you, love? Go and find a drink.' She turned to the man. 'Hello, Den. Lovely to see you.' Andrea followed her guests inside and closed the front door.

Just then, Alan and Chrissie turned into the driveway.

'Have you settled down?' asked Chrissie, 'I hope you're not going to embarrass me. I love Andrea's parties.'

But Alan's attention was distracted. He was staring at Clyde, whose skateboard came skidding to a halt nearby. 'Hey, Clyde!' he called.

Clyde squinted back, confused. It seemed to Alan as if the lad didn't recognise him, yet they knew one another well.

'Er... hello?' said Clyde, tentatively.

'Have you come to see Maria?' Alan asked.

'Sorry, don't know any Maria's.'

'Then why are you here?'

Chrissie gave her ex-husband a dig in the ribs with her elbow. 'Don't be so rude,' she hissed through clenched teeth.

'Andrea's birthday,' replied Clyde. 'My mum's at

work so she sent me round with a card. Is there a problem?'

Alan pressed on, determined to make Clyde remember. 'We bumped into you in the park yesterday evening...'

'Alan!' Chrissie said. 'Leave the boy alone!'

'Please!' appealed Alan, ignoring her. 'You must remember.'

'I was skateboarding yesterday, but on my own.' Clyde frowned at him. 'You're a bit weird,' he said, and quickly sidled past them and up to the front door, glancing back nervously as he went.

'Look at yourself!' urged Chrissie. 'Harassing strangers in the street! Are you going crazy?' She moved off.

'I think I'm the only sane one,' said Alan, to himself.

Sarah Jane appeared out of the mist. 'I take it this is your domain?' she said to the cloaked figure before her. 'Who are you?'

'Nobody,' he replied, in a gravely voice. 'I am nothing.'

'Any chance you could be a bit less cryptic?'

'It's hard for me to make you understand. Ephemeral minds are so limited. Behold!'

Sarah Jane stared as the creature pulled back its black hood. She gasped. There was no face, no features, just a puckered mouth containing razor-sharp teeth. It was like nothing she had ever seen before.

'As you can see, I have no self. I exist only to bring disorder. That is my purpose.' He paused. 'I am the Trickster.'

'But why bring disorder?' asked Sarah Jane.

'Chaos is my blood and air and food.' The Trickster pointed a bony finger at her. 'You are the key to that chaos. I have been waiting, searching through time for just the right person, at just the right moment. I took you to aid the coming of darkness.'

Sarah Jane felt her anger rising. She didn't see why she and her friends had to suffer because of the Trickster's need for chaos. 'Where's Luke?' she demanded. 'Where is my son?'

'The Bane never came to Earth in the timeline I have created,' he explained. 'Luke Smith never existed.'

So if the aliens who made her son had not visited the planet, thought Sarah Jane, then Luke had never been created.

'But people who don't exist end up here, don't they? In this nowhere land. So where is he?' Sarah

Jane was itching to do something, to have her revenge on this evil creature. But she was powerless. She clenched her fists tightly and bit her lip. 'I demand to see my son!'

'He is lost, in the forgotten places,' breathed the Trickster, in his hoarse whisper. 'Even further out than you.'

'If I don't exist, and neither do Luke, Maria and the Bane, what about the Slitheen and the Gorgon and the Patriarchs of the Tin Vagabond? I stopped them all from taking over Earth. What happened to them?'

'I turned them all away. All I needed was the meteor.'

'Why?' she asked. 'What's so special about that?'

'Those other species, they invade for profit, power, revenge. But the meteor is pure chaos. The destruction of Earth, for no reason at all, just blind chance.' The Trickster chuckled dryly as he spoke, as if relishing every word. 'This is food for me.'

'You'll destroy all life on Earth and you don't even care?' cried Sarah Jane.

'I care about you.' He paused. 'You are so wonderful. Your life was so important. And I found the right moment to snuff it out. With the help of Andrea Yates, of course.'

'Andrea was my friend.'

'She wished to save her own life. I could only remove you with her consent.'

Sarah Jane felt the painful stab of betrayal cut through her body. Why would her friend have been so disloyal to her? She couldn't really have left her to die so that she could live? 'Andrea agreed to it?' she asked, nervously.

'I must go now. Events are moving towards their end.'

'No!' yelled Sarah Jane. 'Don't go!'

'I will return,' echoed the Trickster, 'when Earth is no more. Then I will explore your potential further. In particular your memories of this... Doctor.'

'You leave him alone!'

'I can use you to find him. Imagine if the Doctor had never existed. What chaos there would be across the stars!'

'Don't you dare!' shouted Sarah Jane, shaking with rage. The Doctor had been her friend and travelling companion for many years. She'd loved him and treasured the memories of the times and places they'd shared. She wasn't letting the Trickster get his chaos-making hands on him. 'Don't you dare!' she repeated, this time through gritted teeth.

But the Trickster had already disappeared into

the endless whiteness of limbo.

The living room at number thirteen was crowded with guests chatting to one another, sipping wine and helping themselves to plates of sandwiches and sausage rolls. Sunlight streamed in through the front windows, lending the room a bright and happy air.

'Oh, that's lovely,' said Andrea, as she opened the birthday card Clyde had handed to her. 'Thank your mum for me. I'm sorry she couldn't make it.'

Clyde smiled shyly and shuffled from one foot to the other. 'Right... I guess I'll be off then.'

'No, no, stick around,' protested the hostess, and she reached for a plate piled high with slices of sponge cake. 'Here – have one of these.'

Clyde's eyes lit up. 'Okay, no complaints from me.' He took two pieces of cake and shovelled them into his mouth.

Andrea smiled at the lad before her attention was diverted, and she waltzed over to the door, still carrying the plate of cake. 'Well, look who's here! Hello, love!' she exclaimed, giving Chrissie a welcoming kiss. Then she spotted Alan. 'More gorgeous every day,' she said, planting a kiss of his cheek. 'If only I was a few years younger!'

'You can have him,' laughed Chrissie, with a dismissive wave of her hand.

Andrea stared at Alan. 'What's the matter? Cat got your tongue?' she teased.

He stared back, a little coldly, Andrea thought. 'You could say that,' he eventually replied.

Andrea couldn't understand why he was so distant. Had she done something to offend him? Maybe he and Chrissie had had a row? But the thought vanished when she noticed Clyde leaning over the stereo. 'Don't put on that modern stuff. Let it play.'

Pumping out of the machine was an old Sixties song.

'But this is ancient,' complained Clyde, and he shuffled through the CDs in her small collection.

'Not to me it isn't. It's like yesterday,' said Andrea, feeling the same sad, nostalgic twinge she always felt on her birthday. 'Oh, the Sixties, that was my time.' She sighed. 'I was just a kid back then...'

Maria and Sarah Jane were together once again in limbo. Maria was so happy that her friend had kept her word and had come back. Even if they were to be trapped forever in this strange, timeless place, at least they had one another.

'So the meteor's still coming?' asked Maria, sadly.

Sarah Jane nodded.

'And we can't do anything?'

'There must be something. There's always something.'

'Maybe my dad...' She trailed off when she saw the look on her friend's face.

'What can he do?' sighed Sarah Jane. 'He didn't even remember me.' She paused. 'And now you've been taken out of time, he won't remember you either.'

Maria closed her eyes. To be lost was sad. But to be forgotten – that was horrible.

Alan stood alone at the edge of the party, wondering what to do next. He felt for the strange silver box, which he'd slipped in to his pocket. He made sure no one was looking then took it out and eyed it curiously. He was certain this strange little object held the key to everything.

'You what?' Clyde scoffed into his mobile, distracting Alan from his thoughts. 'Danny, are you serious? All right, I'll check it out. Bye.'

Clyde snapped his phone shut, ran over to the stereo, and turned off the music.

'Oh, Clyde, don't change the CD again,' moaned

Andrea.

'It's my mate, Danny,' he said. 'He reckons there's something big on the news. Can we turn on the telly?'

'You kids and your TV,' scoffed Andrea. 'This is meant to be a party.'

'It won't take a minute,' Clyde assured her, and he grabbed the remote control and switched on the television.

'The huge meteor, which was sighted at 2.15pm, is heading towards Earth at a colossal speed,' announced the newsreader. 'Scientists are stressing that the situation is being closely monitored and there is no need for panic...'

'That's what Danny said!' exclaimed Clyde. 'There's this huge rock heading for Earth. Like in Armageddon.'

The party guests started to chatter uneasily amongst themselves, their voices low and urgent.

Alan felt his heart leap in his chest, and he swallowed hard. 'A meteor?' he murmured. 'Then it's all true.'

'Is it going to hit us?' asked Chrissie.

'Danny said it'll fly past, no worries,' reassured Clyde.

'Well, nothing's going to spoil my birthday!'

said Andrea, firmly. 'We need more glasses.'

'I'll give you a hand,' offered Alan.

'Ooh, Andrea, now's your chance,' teased Chrissie.

'Don't worry, I'll bring him back. If he's good.'

Alan followed Andrea out of the living room and into the kitchen.

'I've got some paper cups somewhere,' she said, under her breath. 'Saves wear and tear.' She rummaged in a cupboard. 'Now... where did I put them?'

'What does the name Maria mean to you?' asked Alan, his tone suddenly serious and urgent.

'Eh?' replied Andrea, casually, and she looked up. 'I don't know. Ave Maria? Maria Callas? Maria who works down the petrol station?' She turned away and carried on searching through the cupboard. 'Which Maria?'

Alan was convinced she was hiding something. Her tone was just too casual, too innocent. 'My daughter Maria!' He couldn't disguise his anger any more. 'Where is she?'

'I don't know what you mean.'

'I think you do! You remember! And so do I!' he barked. 'And whatever you've done, I'm going to get her back!'

'You mustn't, please.' Andrea's tone changed completely. She was now staring him directly in the eye. She looked sad and sorry, Alan thought. Her mouth turned down at the edges and her eyes blinking like a child's.

'It's you!' he hissed. 'You're at the centre of it all! I know about the accident! I know about Sarah Jane!'

Chapter Nine

The truth

'I don't know what you're talking about,' said Andrea, shaking her head. It was clear her confessional moment had passed, and her face returned to a sweet, if somewhat cold, smile.

Alan had to get her to confess. He now knew for sure that she was lying. 'You came over the road,' he said, and took a step closer, fixing her with a cold stare. 'You got me out of the way. Then the next minute she was gone.'

'I asked you to help me with my banner, that's all.'

If anything, Alan knew that the silver box he had in his pocket would prove he was on to her. He pulled it out and held it up to the light so she could take a good, long look.

'Where did you get that?' Andrea asked, tensing. 'What have you done with her?'

'The whole world's forgotten her. Now it's your word against mine.' Andrea suddenly changed again to the cool, calm villain he'd seen for a moment earlier. A confession at last? So she did have something to do with his daughter's disappearance. 'But I haven't forgotten,' hissed Alan, through gritted teeth. 'This box, it protected Maria, and now it's protected me.'

'I was going to forget,' said Andrea, her face now falling and her eyes filling with tears. 'He promised me. One night's sleep and I'd have forgotten her.'

'Who?' demanded Alan. 'Who promised you?' He was so close to finding the truth. 'Come on, tell me! Where is she?' he yelled.

'You'd never believe me.'

'I think I would. Andrea, please. Tell me.'

'It was years ago,' said Andrea, as she sat down on a stool in the attic. 'I was thirteen. But I thought I was so grown up. I thought I knew it all. Indestructible, that's what I was. And I had this friend...' She trailed off. The tears were welling up and she was finding it hard to remember her old school friend. She looked up at Alan who was sitting a few feet away, his arms folded. 'Oh, Alan, I'm so sorry. I had this friend called Sarah Jane Smith...'

Andrea's mind drifted back to the summer of

1964. She remembered that boring geography field trip to Westport, and how the two of them had raced down the pier, looking for adventure, ignoring all the warning signs.

'If we've come all the way to the seaside,' Andrea recalled herself shouting, 'then I wanna see the flamin' sea!'

Sarah Jane had protested, of course. She always did. She was so much more sensible than Andrea. 'We're due back at the bus soon,' she'd pointed out. 'And we still haven't been round the museum. Jeffers will skin us!'

But Andrea had ignored her friend. She wanted some fun. Always in pursuit of fun, that was Andrea. Nothing stood in her way when it came to having a good time.

'We larked about on the pier for a bit,' she told Alan. 'Then I went to the edge. There was nothing there...'

She remembered how she had rushed to the very end of the pier, wanting to be as far out to sea as possible. However, as she'd raced towards the railings, they hadn't stopped her as she'd expected them to, but had given way, and she had fallen.

Andrea could still feel what it was like to have nothing beneath her feet, just the cold breeze streaming against her bare legs, making her dress fly up. And she remembered how her stomach had felt – queasy and full – and how she wanted to scream out, but she couldn't.

She told Alan how relieved she had been when she had managed to grab hold of something – a piece of metal jutting out from the girders that supported the pier. And all she could hear was Sarah Jane's screams and her name being called over and over again. But she couldn't reply. She was too terrified to make a sound. It had felt like being in one of those dreams where you desperately want to cry out, but nothing will come out of your mouth.

'Andrea, grab my hand!' her friend had shouted. 'Grab my hand, Andrea! Grab my hand! Come on, Andrea!'

Andrea remembered how she felt her sweaty palms starting to lose grip on the metal, and how she couldn't reach up to where Sarah Jane was leaning forward trying to help her. All she could do was cling on for her life. But even that wasn't working.

'I tried and tried, but I couldn't hold on,' she told Alan, the tears tracing a path down her cheeks as she remembered that terrible day all those years ago. 'But then I heard this voice... "You don't have to die," it called. "I can save you. Someone has to fall, but it doesn't have to be you. You only have to agree. Let her die in your place.'''

Andrea couldn't look Alan in the eye. She let her gaze fall to the floor. 'I felt my fingers slipping. I couldn't hang on any longer. So I said yes.'

Andrea buried her face in her hands, ashamed to be telling her neighbour this story. It was a terrible thing to admit to, but she had to unburden herself to someone.

'After that, I found myself back on the pier. I was safe,' she confessed, after a pause. 'It was Sarah Jane who was dangling from the pier now.'

She remembered how confusing it had been at the time. One second she was about to die, the next it was her friend who was in deadly danger. How had it happened? It was like a crazy dream – a nightmare. She was relieved it wasn't her any more, but terrified for Sarah Jane. Would she be blamed for this? Had she made it happen?

'Andrea! Help me!' her friend had screamed. 'Help me!'

'What happened?' Andrea remembered calling, confused. 'Sarah Jane, take my hand! Take my hand!

But her friend couldn't reach. And in what felt like both a split second and an eternity, she watched

Sarah Jane Smith fall into the deep, grey water. Gone forever.

'She was just a kid,' sobbed Andrea.

'What happened then?' asked Alan.

'This is the strangest part. I looked up and there was this tall figure in a black cloak. He had no face.' She paused. 'He gave me a box. Just like yours. He told me that I'd forget what had happened. But regardless of whether I was awake or asleep, he said he'd always be with me. Whoever he is.'

Andrea explained that she had passed out after that, and when she awoke, the figure was gone. 'I remembered the accident, but he made me forget everything else.'

She reached behind her, and from a pile of junk, pulled out her own version of the silver box. She held it up. 'I never knew how I got this. But, somehow, I knew I couldn't throw it away.' Andrea paused and dried her eyes with a tissue. 'Then when Maria came over this morning shouting about Sarah Jane, it all came back. The voice, the deal I made – '

'Sacrificing your friend to save your own life!' broke in Alan, with a bitter edge to his voice.

'I was thirteen. I was terrified,' replied Andrea, struggling to defend herself. 'Can you imagine what it's like – to know you're going to die? To feel the end of everything closing in on you?' She stared at Alan, hoping he'd understand. But his cold expression told her he had no sympathy for what she'd done. 'Why am I even asking? I'm the only person alive who could possibly know.'

She started to cry again.

'She was your friend!'

'And I loved her!

'Yeah, right,' Alan scoffed.

'I did!' said Andrea, firmly, seeing the disgusted frown on his face. 'Don't look at me like that!'

Andrea thought back on what Sarah Jane had been like when they were at school together. 'Oh, she was funny. I used to crack up. The things she said. She was clever, not swotty. In class she didn't even have to try.'

Andrea paused and turned away. 'I had to do it. I had to survive.'

'And the minute you remembered, you did it again. Today. To Maria.' Alan shook his head disapprovingly. 'If I didn't have this box I would've forgotten my own daughter.'

'I had to send her away,' said Andrea, knowing she'd done the wrong thing.

'What could Maria do to you?'

'She made me remember. She made me face

what I did.'

Andrea crossed the room, sobbing as she went, and stood in front of the dusty mirror. Its dim glass showed Alan's reflection. Then beside him there suddenly appeared the hooded figure of the Trickster.

'What do you want me to do?' asked the black-cowled shape.

Andrea looked at Alan. He hadn't heard the voice, nor could he see what she could see. 'And yes, now I've done it again – sent your daughter away,' she told him, sadly. 'And how can I face that?'

'I can send him away too, but you must agree,' said the Trickster, in his eerie whisper.

'I agree! I agree!' said Andrea, to the creature in the mirror.

'Agree to what?' asked Alan, confused.

'I'm so sorry...' said Andrea, and she moved quickly over to Alan and knocked the silver box out of his hand. It clattered to the floor, and at the same time there was a flash of brilliant blue light and the Graske appeared out of nowhere. The creature gave a chilling growl and lunged for Alan.

Alan leapt up, dodged it and raced out of the room.

The Graske raced after him.

Chapter Ten

The meteor approaches

'The meteor is on a collision course with Britain, but the RAF has released a statement saying they are confident it can be shot down,' proclaimed the newsreader. 'The missiles are already being prepared.'

'This is amazing!' Clyde gasped, as he and the other party guests stared in disbelief at the TV screen.

'Oh, let the Army deal with it,' said Chrissie, dismissively. 'It's what they get paid for.' She paused. 'I wonder what's keeping Alan.'

Chrissie pushed past the guests and went out into the hallway. At that moment, her ex-husband came tearing down the stairs, dashed straight past her and careered out through the front door.

Before she had time to call after him, something even more bizarre happened. A tiny, hideous-looking creature came thumping down the stairs after him. It growled at Chrissie then scurried after Alan.

'Well, that's just ridiculous,' she snorted.

Out on Bannerman Road, the Graske surveyed his surroundings, sniffing the air. Everywhere was silent. There was no one in sight.

Just then, with a screeching of rubber against tarmac, Alan came skateboarding round the corner at tremendous speed.

The Graske barely had time to register the figure sailing towards him, let alone dodge out of the way, and he was knocked off his feet and onto the hard ground.

'I'm telling you,' huffed Chrissie, as she returned to the living room, 'my ex-husband and a dwarf in a suit! Now I've seen it all!'

'Just shut up and listen!' ordered Clyde.

'The meteor is now approximately ten minutes from impact,' said the newsreader. 'But... hold on...

we have some breaking news.' He put a finger to his earpiece. 'I'm being told... it's been confirmed... I'm sorry.' His voice took on a grave tone. 'The missile strike has failed.'

'It's gonna hit us!' yelled Clyde, horrified. 'It's going to blow up Earth!'

Andrea entered the room and stared at the TV screen.

Outside there was a deep, sinister rumbling. It was the meteor entering Earth's atmosphere. The massive ball of rock was sending out powerful vibrations that were starting to shake the entire house.

'Can you hear it?' yelled Clyde. 'That's it!' He raced out of the room.

Chrissie and the other guests quickly followed him, chattering worriedly amongst themselves.

Only Andrea remained behind. 'But it can't be...' she murmured to herself. 'Why's this happening now?' She ran out through the front door and joined the others on Bannerman Road.

People from neighbouring houses were also out on the street. Every one of them was staring up at the sky, their mouths wide open, expressions of disbelief plastered across their faces.

'There it is!' called Clyde, pointing up at the sky.

Thundering towards them, growing bigger by the second, was a vast ball of rock, clearly scorching hot, and spewing out clouds of black gas.

'They'll find a way to deal with it,' said Clyde, shakily. 'They've got to.'

'That's real though!' said Chrissie. 'There's no way of stopping it now!'

'Maria said, "Sarah Jane can stop the meteor",' Andrea muttered, under her breath.

But no one heard her...

Alan had dragged the semiconscious Graske into the living room of number thirty-six. Having tied the creature up with some rope he kept under the stairs, Alan straddled him, making sure he was unable to escape. 'You took my daughter!' he shouted.

'Set me free!' growled the Graske, struggling to shake off his bonds.

'Bring her back!' demanded Alan as he stared at this creature he could hardly believe in. What was it? An alien? A sprite? A dream? No, this was real enough, Alan thought to himself. 'Where is she?'

'I must be free! I must move! I cannot be still or I will die!'

'Then tell me where you took Maria!'

'He said to take her,' snarled the creature. 'I must

do as he says.'

'Why?'

'He is the Trickster. He waits outside Time. To bring chaos.'

The Graske tried again to wriggle free of the ropes, but Alan just held him down with greater force. He was determined to get an answer, to find out where his daughter had been taken. 'That meteor is coming in. It means the end of the world. The end of you, too.'

'You people are stupid – you don't matter.'

'And you're so clever you let yourself become a slave?'

'A Graske is never enslaved!'

'You look pretty tied up to me,' said Alan.

'Must be free!' The Graske wriggled frantically, gnashing its pointed little teeth as it did so.

'Then show me how to get Maria back!' demanded Alan. 'Now!'

'The snare will retrieve her,' the Graske spat out, after a pause. 'Then you set me free!'

Alan spotted something attached to the creature's belt. It was a strange, alien-looking gun. He pulled it out and examined it. 'Is this what you mean?'

The Graske grunted an affirmation.

Alan held up the device and looked it over

carefully. It was like nothing he'd ever seen before. He pressed a hexagonal button on the side, and he felt a strange shock of energy pulse through the device. The room seemed to vibrate for a moment, and when he looked around him, all the photographs of Maria had reappeared.

Then, with a flash of blue light, Maria herself appeared.

Alan was so relieved. 'Maria!' he shouted, and they ran into one another's arms and hugged.

'Dad! You're a genius!'

'No, no, no, listen!' stammered Alan. 'The meteor, you were right, it's heading straight for us!'

'We can stop it,' said Maria. 'But we need Sarah Jane.'

'I don't remember Sarah Jane.'

'Dad, trust me! You remembered me when I disappeared, yeah? Well, I remember Sarah Jane. And she's the only person who can save us!'

'How?' asked Alan. 'She's just a normal woman, isn't she?'

'She's a lot more than that. Now – you've got to help me. We can get Sarah Jane back. Whatever you did with that thing,' she said, pointing at the gun, 'do it again!'

Alan aimed the device at the ceiling and pushed

the button. But nothing happened this time. Sarah Jane did not appear.

'I got put back here – where I belong,' mused Maria. 'She'll be where she belongs.' She paused. 'Her attic!'

Maria and her dad raced out of the room, leaving the Graske alone.

He shook himself from side to side, making growling noises all the while, struggling to break the ropes. Eventually, with a massive heave, they snapped and he was free. He then clambered to his feet and teleported away.

Out on Bannerman Road people were running, screaming, dashing about, as the meteor barrelled ever closer to them.

'Mum!' called Maria, as she raced out of the house.

'Oh, it's too late, sweetheart!' cried Chrissie. 'It's too late for all of us! I'm sorry for all the times I let you down and all the – '

'Not now!' Maria pushed past her mum and dashed into number thirteen.

Alan raced in after her.

Chapter Eleven

The return

Andrea stood alone in the attic. 'Please!' she begged, holding the silver box at arm's length. 'You saved me once before - you can do it again.' She paused, shook her head despairingly and closed her eyes. 'Please!'

Nothing happened. She opened them again and looked around her. Something caught her eye. Something in the mirror.

'No...' she murmured. 'Not you...'

It was Sarah Jane Smith.

'Andrea Yates,' she called, her voice sad, distant and echoing. 'It's you. All grown up.'

Andrea turned pale. She realised who it was. Her old school friend. The one she hadn't seen in more than forty years. But she wasn't a child any more

– she was an adult, as old as she was. 'Well, look at you,' she said, with a sneer. 'Scrubbed up well. But then you always did look younger than you were.'

Andrea paused to think. Her face darkened. 'But you can't be here!' she cried, realising it wasn't possible for them both to exist. 'Not while I'm here! You can't come back!'

Just then the attic door flew open and Maria and Alan burst in.

'Sarah Jane!' called Maria, as she caught sight of her friend trapped inside the mirror.

'That's her?' asked Alan, still carrying the Graske's device. 'But she's only in the mirror. This thing didn't work.'

'I can't get back while Andrea's here,' called Sarah Jane. 'And I must get back – to save Luke. To save the world!'

'So what do we do?' asked Maria, desperately.

'There is a way,' said Sarah Jane, solemnly, looking Andrea in the eye. 'It's why the Trickster got rid of Maria. Because she was the one who confronted you – and she might have persuaded you to go back on your deal. This whole thing depends on your agreement to my death, all those years ago.'

'If you break off the deal,' shouted Maria, 'Sarah Jane will come back. All you have to do is pull out of it, say no.'

'I can't!' spat Andrea.

'If you don't, that meteor's going to hit!' joined in Alan. 'Is that what you want?'

'I'm sorry, Andrea, but you were meant to die!' cried Maria, angrily.

'Meant? Who says I'm meant to die?' Andrea was shaking with rage now. 'I was so young. I had so much to do. And I did it. Look at me. I lived – every single moment. Because I knew what it was worth.'

'So did I!' yelled Sarah Jane.

Andrea turned around and faced the mirror. 'And you're the chosen one? The golden girl?' she asked, sarcastically.

'Nobody was chosen. It was stupid and pointless, what happened that day. But this is worse. The Trickster twisted it – he used you.'

'So I die... at thirteen?'

'And my son gets a chance to live. He's lost out there, Andrea, somewhere terrible. And I'm begging you – please save him.'

'If I do, what happens to my life?' asked Andrea, tears welling in the corners of her eyes. 'All the things I did as I grew up – they get scrubbed out? I get forgotten?'

Andrea thought back across her fifty-six years. She remembered all the amazing things she'd done. With incredible clarity she saw herself passing her driving test, getting into art college, the first painting she ever sold, her holiday to Kenya, the night her mother died... it was all as vivid as if it had happened only yesterday.

'You were never forgotten. Never.' Sarah Jane's voice brought her back to the present. 'What I saw that day, it changed me forever. I saw how precious life is. And it made me fight to defend it – across all these years. Because of you, Andrea.' Her voice quivered, almost breaking up. 'It was all because of you. My best friend.'

Suddenly Andrea shuddered and turned around. There was the Trickster, shrouded in his long, black cloak, standing at the back of the attic.

'Is that him?' asked Alan. 'Is that the Trickster?' He headed angrily for the creature, as if he was going to lash out at him.

'Dad, no! Don't go near him!' Maria shrieked, and she grabbed hold of her dad's T-shirt and held him back.

'Andrea Yates!' called the Trickster, in an echoing voice. 'They want to kill you all over again. Remember your bargain with me.'

Andrea slowly walked over to the shadowy form and looked him directly in the face – or, at least, where his face should have been. She shook her head sadly, her voice choked with tears. 'You tricked me! You used a child! And now you're destroying Earth!'

'Chaos is good,' he said.

'Well, I say no,' hissed Andrea, defiantly. 'If there's one thing I can do with my life, it's put a stop to you – for good!' Andrea took a deep breath. 'I've changed my mind,' she said. 'I'm taking the deal back!'

'Then you die!' bellowed the Trickster, cruelly.

'I've been dead for over forty years.'

Andrea turned her back on him and headed for the mirror. She stared sadly at her old friend. 'It's been a good life... it's my birthday today...' She paused for a moment, then smiled. 'Goodbye, Sarah Jane. I'm going now. And you're free!'

And with tears falling down her face, Andrea threw the silver box at the mirror and the glass shattered into hundreds of pieces.

The Trickster let out a terrible scream and vanished from the room.

And so did Andrea Yates.

Back in 1964, it was no longer Sarah Jane gripping onto the pier for dear life, but Andrea once again. History had been returned to its original course.

The young Sarah Jane leaned over the edge, trying frantically to grasp her friend's hand. 'Andrea!' she yelled. 'Grab my hand! Grab my hand! Andrea!'

Andrea looked up at her friend. 'Remember me,' she whispered, then her grip loosened and she fell down, down, down into the murky sea.

'No-ooooooo!' cried Sarah Jane.

But it was too late.

In the attic, in the present day, Sarah Jane, Maria, Alan and Luke all fell to the floor.

'I'm back!' laughed Sarah Jane.

'We're all back!' Maria looked around her. The attic had returned to how it used to be – cluttered with strange alien technology, books, memorabilia, and all the things that only Sarah Jane could have. She let out a long sigh of relief.

'Back where we belong!' Sarah Jane grinned at her friends – and they grinned back.

'That felt like a spatio-temporal shift caused by extra-quantum forces,' said Luke, proudly.

'In English?' asked Alan.

'Oh, it's all back to normal!' laughed Maria. Then

she remembered something that made her stomach leap up into her mouth. 'The meteor!'

'It's still coming!' cried Sarah Jane.

'Thirty seconds till impact!' added Luke.

'Mr Smith, I need you!'

Sarah Jane, Luke and Maria raced over to the brick chimney breast that concealed the computer. With big puffs of steam and the noise of a jet engine firing up, Mr Smith emerged, his lights flashing frantically. 'Emergency measures required,' he said.

'Luke – steady the magnetic buffer!' ordered Sarah Jane.

Luke threw a large lever forward. 'Done!'

'Come on!' called Maria, knowing there was next to no time before the meteor crashed into them, obliterating the planet totally.

'Right, Mr Smith,' said Sarah Jane. 'Activate!'

The computer's screen filled with statistics and calculations as he strained to deflect the meteor.

Maria closed her eyes and hoped that if she used all her willpower too, they could stop the rock from hitting Earth. But she also knew it would take more than just willpower...

Out on Bannerman Road, Chrissie, Clyde and their neighbours cowered in the shadow of the burning ball of rock as it roared towards them.

It was so close now that they could feel its heat. Everything was getting darker and darker as it blocked out the light from the sun, and tiny pieces of ash and fragments of rock were raining down on them. The air stank and if you inhaled too deeply your lungs were filled with fumes.

Clyde crouched down, his arms wrapped around him and his face covered.

Chrissie simply closed her eyes, clasped her hands together and let out a long breath.

But then a miracle happened. Just as the massive meteor was about to crash into the ground, it suddenly turned, passed over their heads and blazed back out into space.

The crowd on the street stared up at the flaming ball as it dwindled back into the late afternoon sky.

The air was now filled with the sound of cheering, and people were running about, embracing one another.

The cheering made Clyde look up, and what he saw changed his expression from fear to relief and then delight. 'She did it!' he yelled, at the top of his voice. 'She did it!' And he jumped up and down on the spot in triumph.

Chrissie opened her eyes, but remained rooted

to the spot. Then after a long pause she spoke. 'Oh, like Bobby Sue had anything to do with that!' she scoffed. But she couldn't help grinning, too, happy to be alive. 'You'll be telling me she invented the zip next!'

But Clyde wasn't listening. He was still leaping about, making whooping noises. 'Come here!' he called, and he grabbed Chrissie by the waist and they span around together in circles, laughing and cheering.

In the attic, Sarah Jane and Maria were also dancing for joy. Luke looked on, smiling.

'Meteor K67 has been deflected,' said Mr Smith.

'Yes! We did it!' cried Sarah Jane, and she threw her arms around her son. 'But never mind that – you're back!'

'Was I away?' asked Luke, innocently.

'Yes, but you're never, ever, ever, ever, ever, ever going away again!'

'But what happened?' Luke looked confused.

'A friend of mine just saved the world,' said Sarah Jane, a proud smile on her face. 'Her name was Andrea Yates.'

Just then the attic door burst open and Clyde raced in. 'Oh, that was brilliant!' he shouted. 'We did it! You should have seen it out there...' He trailed off as he caught sight of Alan. 'What's he doing here?'

Everyone turned and stared at Maria's dad.

Alan was standing quietly in the corner, a baffled, frightened expression on his face.

'Aliens? Monsters? Supercomputers?' he said. 'Is anyone going to tell me what's going on?'

It hadn't occurred to Maria for one second that her dad was now standing in Sarah Jane's secret attic – a place he was never supposed to see. In all the confusion to stop Andrea, she hadn't even thought about telling him not to follow her upstairs. He now knew things he wasn't meant to know – that there was alien life all around them, and that she, Sarah Jane and their friends had been facing it every day.

'Come on!' he demanded. 'I need some answers!' He paused and stared from one to the other, his gaze finally resting on Maria. 'Who's going first?'

Epilogue

Maria and Alan left number thirteen and wandered down the driveway. It was still light, though the sun was making its way slowly down towards the horizon.

Maria couldn't believe that only hours before she hadn't existed. Time had been changed and her entire life had vanished and been instantly forgotten – even by those she loved the most, and who loved her.

And she wasn't the only one. Sarah Jane, her dearest friend, had disappeared, too. All her life after the age of thirteen had evaporated. And what would Maria do without Sarah Jane? She would never have had all the adventures they'd had, would never have met creatures from another world, never felt like she mattered so much. And she did matter, she knew that.

Still, Andrea had done the right thing in the end and sacrificed herself. After all, in a funny kind of way, she had had the best of both worlds. In Andrea's mind she had lived all those years, she hadn't died in 1964. Strangely, she'd cheated time. But it was all too complicated to think about. Maria decided if she kept going her head might explode.

She sighed. Everything was back to normal now. Well, almost normal. There was, however, one tiny problem. Her dad.

Sarah Jane had said that now he'd seen the attic and the aliens, it was best if Maria explained everything to him. And it was only right to come from her. After all, she knew him better than anyone.

Sarah Jane had also said there was no point in simplifying the truth or skipping the tricky bits. Her friend had been clear about this. Alan had seen what he'd seen – in fact, without his help Earth would have been destroyed – and there was no point keeping all the facts from him.

But where should she begin, pondered Maria? How to explain this amazing world she'd found herself at the very centre of, since they had moved to Bannerman Road? It wasn't going to be easy.

Still, there was a part of Maria that was relieved.

At last she could be honest about her life. She could share those things that were most important to her with her dad. They'd be on the same footing, able to support one another, confide in one another. Just like a father and daughter ought to.

Maria smiled up at her dad as they walked down the path to their own house and Alan opened the front door.

Though it wouldn't be easy, she just knew everything would be all right in the end. Tomorrow would be a whole new day and, no doubt, a whole new adventure.

Only this time they'd face it together.

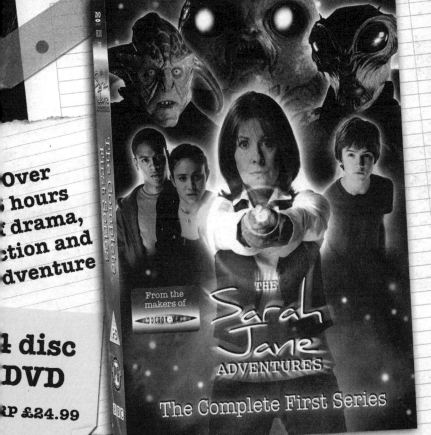

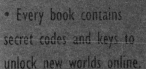